REVENGE
IS
COMING

BOOK THREE OF
THE PROMISES SERIES

AFTER THE VIETNAM
WAR NOVEL

GLYN HAYNIE

Revenge is Coming: After the Vietnam War Novel

For information about this title or to order other books and/or electronic media, contact the publisher:

Glyn Haynie
www.glynhaynie.net
glyn@glynhaynie.com

ISBNs:
Hardback: 978-1-7340260-6-1
Paperback: 978-1-7340260-7-8
e-book: 978-1-7340260-9-2

Printed in the United States of America.

Typesetting: ebooklaunch.com
Final Proof Editor: Cindy Draughon
Copy Editor: Keith Gordon
Editor: Annie J from Just Copyeditors
Cover Designer: Suzette Vaughn
Author Photograph: Shannon Prothro Photography

Books by Glyn Haynie

Revenge is Coming
After the Vietnam War Novel (Book 3)

Return to the Madness
A Vietnam War Novel (Book 2)

Promises to the Fallen
A Vietnam War Novel (Book 1)

When I Turned Nineteen
A Vietnam War Memoir

Soldiering After the Vietnam War
Changed Soldiers in a Changed Country

Finding My Platoon Brothers
Vietnam Then and Now

CONTENTS

REVENGE

IS

COMING

PROLOGUE

Chu Lai, Republic of Vietnam - July 1970

The military policeman's hand clamped hard around Lieutenant *Bảo Đặng's* shoulder. He steered him in cold silence toward the open door of a cell containing seven other prisoners of war.

Without warning, the MP suddenly let him go and shoved him forward. Dang jolted inward, stumbling and confused.

Once the door slammed shut, the new Viet Cong prisoner turned to face his fellow inmates. On the right side of Dang's face, a blood-soaked bandage concealed the knife wound that Sergeant Eddie Henderson had inflicted upon him the day the Americans captured him. The wound was still open, bleeding and oozing, the same way his brain felt.

Dang glowered at the other Viet Cong and NVA soldiers as he made his way into the expansive room. The floor creaked as he stepped forward, cautious and unsure. The other captives didn't attempt to make eye contact with him. They looked down, looked away, looked sideways. They pretended to examine and pick at their clothing—anything but look at him.

With a scowl, Dang stopped near a bunk and stood over an old man who sat quietly on one end of the bed, subdued and meek. Within seconds, the man rose and shuffled away, leaving the cot to the officer.

After he lay on the bed, Dang stroked the bandage that covered the wound, attempting to piece together what happened, to put everything into context.

When searched, the guard's deft hands seemed to go every-where on Dang's tense body, into all of the folds of the fabric, up, down, reaching and searching. But they still didn't find the picture of Henderson's wife he had hidden away.

He pulled the photograph out of his shirt pocket and stared at her. With a twisted smile spreading across his face, he slid the photo back into its hiding place.

Dang remembered shooting the giant American soldier. Then he fought Henderson. The memory of Henderson on top of him, slashing at his face with a large knife filled his heart with hatred.

That was when he'd pulled his pistol, shooting Henderson in the stomach. But the black soldier, Johnston, had stopped him from killing Henderson outright.

This was when the rest of the Americans had shown up, capturing him.

Dang's face flushed as his body shook with anger. His embarrassment was absolute. Utter humiliation . . .

Yes, humiliation burned now in his mind with the recollection of that moment of torment—of frustrated, shameful, infuriating defeat.

Later the next afternoon, an interpreter called out for the lieutenant to approach the door of the prison cell. Dang had known him before he'd surrendered to the Americans, and they had acknowledged each other when the MP led him to his cell.

The man had become a guard and interpreter at the prisoner-of-war compound in Chu Lai. The Americans called the soldiers that surrendered *Chiêu Hồi*. Well, Dang had no respect for these men. But he was willing to use the interpreter to escape.

After talking to the interpreter for several minutes, he made a deal for his freedom. Dang reached into the depths of his jacket pocket to bring out a precious Seiko watch. He eyed it for a second and ran his rough thumb over its glass face as if giving it a silent, fond goodbye.

Then he handed it silently to the interpreter.

The watch had belonged to Ray Laurel, and *Cánh* had slipped it to Dang this morning along with a Zippo cigarette lighter when he was exercising near the fence. These two items were special to him.

No more than three hours later, the interpreter escorted Dang from his cell. The night sky was dark as they walked from one building to another.

Saying nothing whatsoever and giving only the occasional nod to indicate where Dang was to head next, the interpreter escorted him to the clinic to get the wound on his face treated by a doctor. That was their first stop.

Dang flinched as the doctor carefully scraped away the pus and rancid flesh and then filled the deep cut with an iodine compound before stitching the wound closed and taping on a fresh new dressing.

The interpreter's head flicked again, to the side now, indicating a rear door for him to move through. The motion made it clear that Dang should do it fast.

Not a word was exchanged between the two men as Dang slipped past him.

The interpreter led Dang to the rear of the compound. This was the darkest area of the prison. The man's hand pointed downward, and Dang could almost make out the shadows of the night and a patch of—somehow—an even deeper blackness where there must've been a gap in the tall perimeter fence, maybe a hole or a section removed.

He was showing him where to slip underneath.

One word, barely audible, "*Đi.*" *Go.*

Dang gave a quick nod of his own, then hunkered down onto his belly, crawling, and disappeared off into the jungle accompanied only by the myriad sounds of the restless nighttime, alive with chirping insects.

•

It was days before April 30, 1975, that Dang presented himself as a South Vietnamese colonel with his wife, *Lài*, and aide, *Cánh*, and boarded a flight to America with hundreds of other refugees bound for California.

He believed that the new government of unified Vietnam wouldn't approve of his actions during the war. Therefore, he simply fled.

In Berkeley he had a brief encounter with Henderson. One evening, not long after he arrived in America, Dang observed him sitting with his wife at a restaurant. He took that opportunity to torment Henderson and his wife, letting them know he was now in the States.

Dang thought of killing Henderson right there in public, but decided against it. He had only arrived recently in his new country and didn't want to create a mess for himself—something that would follow him like another unholy nightmare.

A year later, he left California for Houston, Texas, where he came to settle in the Little Saigon district that felt a tiny bit like home.

It didn't take him long to find strange alliances with the area's underworld, too, and he quickly assumed a position of influence, even rigging the election to become the Union boss of the Vietnamese fishermen. The more power he acquired, the stronger he became in the community—and the more people looked up to him.

With deep scars running down both sides of his face, he presented an intimidating image, and Dang knew how to use fear to motivate anyone who dared to disobey him.

During the war he'd killed many villagers and soldiers who wouldn't do as instructed, and he wouldn't hesitate to do the same in his new country. He'd taken to killing like a duck takes to water.

Dang decided to use his skills to enforce his personalized brand of law within the Vietnamese community, and word spread quickly of his deeds as a Viet Cong lieutenant during what the Vietnamese commonly referred to as the American War. He remembered the villagers he massacred, the boys and girls he ripped from their mothers' arms to serve him, and how he had stolen the only food they had.

He was as ruthless to his own people as he'd been to the Americans.

His gang forced the union workers to pay "insurance," otherwise something might happen to their boats. The waters around these parts were notorious, he said to them, and about anything might come to pass, such as boats getting oddly cast adrift after nightfall or go missing together with their ropes—or even found with hacked-out holes in their sides.

So, a little protection was always advisable if the fishermen were wise and if they understood what was good for them.

The fishermen did understand.

Dang surrounded himself with his second in command, Canh, and three other ex-soldiers. They ran the Vietnamese fishing industry. Through Dang's intimidation, the residents of Little Saigon wouldn't go to the local police for help, nor would they assist the police in any investigation.

"I can build another boat," one would say quietly, looking down.

"My boat, I gave it to my friend," offered another, almost tearful, knowing what had happened to his handmade boat. "No matter . . ."

But while all of this was happening, Dang's old familiar hatred toward the American, Sergeant Eddie Henderson, never dwindled. He thought daily about killing that man for disfiguring his face, escaping from captivity, disgracing him, and then capturing him and locking him in an accursed, foul-smelling, cockroach-infested prison cell.

A NEWSPAPER STORY

Austin, Texas - August 1980

Not more than two hours after he'd fallen asleep, Eddie Henderson tossed and rolled as if running for his life through the jungle.

He whimpered in his sleep. "Ray, follow me!"

Eddie flipped onto his stomach and crawled toward the foot of the bed.

"Let's go, Ray! C'mon!"

When Eddie slid to the floor, he yelled, "Run, it's fucking Dang! He's comin' for us!" His legs moved in a frantic sprint.

Sweat soaked his body, and he shook violently. He watched Laurel stare into the barrel of the pistol and say, "Gawddamn it!"

Eddie's heart was beating hard against his chest, thumping on his ribcage.

"I'm going to fucking kill you!" he screamed at Dang.

"Eddie . . . Eddie . . . it's okay." Eddie felt Cheryl, his wife of ten years, stroke his arm. "It's a dream. I have you. You're safe."

She helped Eddie back into bed, whispering to him all the while.

Curling up next to him, Cheryl murmured again, stroking his hair, "It's okay. It's okay. I'm with you now."

Eddie laid there, eyes wide, pupils like pinpricks. The nightmares were always the same. He felt paralyzed and frustrated by the memories he couldn't control, the ones that came after him, seeking him out. Eventually, he rolled out of bed and padded toward the kitchen.

•

When Eddie recognized the face in the picture on the community page of the Austin American-Statesman newspaper, his body reacted instantly. His hands started to shake. He set down his mug to avoid sloshing any coffee onto the table as he stared at the man in the photo. He could feel the fear and hatred surface as beads of sweat formed and rolled down his forehead.

Dang!

Dang was staring back at him, for God's sake.

Seeing him in the photograph woke the hatred he felt for Dang, hatred that had stayed dormant the last four years but resurfaced as strong as ever.

He had given up the search for Dang a year after seeing him in Berkeley. And now here he was, on the table, in his own damn house.

Eddie vividly recalled Dang pointing his pistol at Ray Laurel and Ray calling out for help. Eddie had looked on in horror as Dang squeezed the trigger nonchalantly as if he was attempting to take out an apple placed atop a tree stump. Emotionless.

After that, Dang had turned to Eddie, met his gaze, then shrugged as if there was nothing he could've done about it. It was as if taking a man's life in such cold blood was as natural as taking a piss.

But Laurel's dead eyes still haunted him, as did the memory of the bloody fragments of his brain as they'd soaked into the ground, red and creamy gray blobs scattered among the leaves.

It had been horrific, and the metallic scent of blood that filled his nose would never leave his mind.

At that moment he'd told Dang he would avenge the death of Ray Laurel, his friend and fellow squad member.

The words he spoke when Dang fired the pistol rang in his ears. "I'll kill the fucker, Ray. I promise you that! I'll kill the fucker!"

Gripped in panic now, Henderson stood frozen, wanting nothing more than to get to Dang. Sweat covered every inch of his body, and he felt the oxygen pumping inside his lungs but was afraid to exhale.

Revenge was coming.

He didn't care if five years had passed since he'd last seen Dang in Berkeley. The promise he had made to Laurel on the day of the execution—well, it was one he meant to keep.

And he couldn't rest until he kept it.

Eddie's body involuntarily jerked with the same motion as when he'd fought Dang. He smiled as he recalled slicing the right side of Dang's face, carving into it with the knife to produce a scar that matched the left side.

The cut had felt like slicing into a delicate ham joint—only he wished he'd had a serrated blade to make the wound even worse.

He hoped it got infected.

His hand moved to his stomach, stroking the healed bullet hole Dang left when he shot him ten years earlier.

He recalled the morning when Lieutenant Brighton, his platoon leader, and Johnston, Williams, and Little JJ—all squad members— had told him Dang escaped from the prisoner-of-war compound at Chu Lai. Well, fuck that man.

He'd been angry that day. Uncontrollably angry. Seething.

And now his hands trembled as he stared at the newspaper, at the face in the photo that was bringing all of this back now, making him relive each of the heinous acts Dang had committed.

He thought of Dang appearing five years earlier outside the restaurant in Berkeley one evening when he and Cheryl were having dinner. Fear, anger, and the urge to kill had seized him. Dang even taunted Cheryl with her photograph, the same one he'd ripped off Eddie when the Viet Cong captured him.

After the initial shock of seeing Dang outside the restaurant, Eddie made efforts to track him. As the years passed, his attempts to find him eventually faded away, but the nightmares got worse and worse. "And now he's right here—in Texas!"

Hatred erupted in the pit of his stomach. His heart beat faster as sweat trickled from every pore in his body. The thoughts of killing Dang kept coming like waves hitting the shoreline—receding, welling, coming at him all over again, engulfing his whole being.

But now Eddie felt something else.

It was a sense of satisfaction. He knew he had it in him to finish Dang once for all. The time had come—the time for his sweet revenge.

THE MAN FROM THE RESTAURANT

Cheryl walked into the kitchen and flipped her long red hair out of the way so she could button her blouse. "Hurry up. We'll be late for work."

Eddie ran his hand through his hair. "In a minute." He held the paper at an angle to better study the photograph.

Cheryl looked at her husband. "What's wrong? Looks like you've seen a ghost." She put a hand on his shoulder. "Look at me."

Eddie stared into her green eyes. "Check out this picture." He held the photograph for her to see. It was an image of a group of men standing near a fishing vessel tied up alongside a pier.

"I don't see anything. Just a bunch of people around a boat."

"Well, that . . . there!" He jabbed at the paper with his finger. "Look at the man standing on the dock to the rear."

Cheryl grabbed the newspaper. "Let me see." After a moment, she gasped for air. "Oh, my God! It's him." She dropped the paper on the table. "It's the man from the restaurant!"

Eddie's eyes narrowed. "Yes."

The room was quiet as they stood staring at one another.

"So what are you going to do?" Cheryl asked as she slid onto the kitchen chair, her voice sounding as if Eddie had all the answers to something that was pretty much unanswerable.

He stepped behind her and placed a hand on her shoulder, staring out the window at the clear blue sky. "I don't know."

He squeezed her skin softly as if that would reassure her.

Neither of them were comforted. Far from it.

Cheryl faced him.

"Look, you need to call the police and report him."

"What am I supposed to say?" Eddie's forehead wrinkled as his eyebrows came together. "That he's a man who killed people in the war? That he executed Laurel? Look, the police can't do anything to Dang. There's no evidence for any of it, and a hell of a lot of men killed a hell of a lot of other men in the war. That's what war is . . ."

He was getting irritated with her now.

She hated when that happened. Cheryl stood and put her arms around his neck. That always seemed to work.

"I would still tell them anyway. Someone should be able to do something." She sighed. "How about telling the army?"

Now she was becoming a nag.

But it kind of did make sense. At least he'd have done something. Even if that something was a futile waste of time.

"I'll think about it. But I'm not promising anything."

"Oh, Eddie, don't do anything you'll regret." She looked at him with wide eyes. "I don't want you to get hurt. I don't know what I—what we would do without you, Eddie . . . Me and the boys and little Ray."

She sure knew how to soften him. There was no way he wanted to get hurt either, leaving her and his family in that kind of fucked-up mess.

He didn't need to tell Cheryl that he would probably kill the man. She knew it already, and it passed unspoken between them.

The hatred he carried for Dang was eating through his soul. His only thought was that he wanted him dead. Eddie didn't care how he did it, whether with a bullet through the head, or with his bare hands choking him to death, or thrusting a knife into his heart, or pushing him over a cliff. The how didn't matter. Only that it happened somehow—and soon.

"He doesn't deserve to be in the States. That son of a bitch doesn't deserve to live." His eyes lit up as he anticipated the taste of revenge. "Damn it. I promised Laurel I'd do it if I ever got a chance. Sure as hell I would. As sure as the sun shines in the—"

"Take some time to think it through." She touched his hand. "Please, call the police before you do anything. Promise me—"

"I'm not promising anything right now."

He turned to leave the kitchen. "I need to get ready for work."

•

Cheryl picked up Mitch and sat him on her lap. "Good morning, sweetheart. I'll make you breakfast."

"Mommy, I want Fruit Loops." Mitch gave his mother a big wet kiss on the cheek as he twirled his little hands through her hair and messed it up.

"Fruit Loops it is." She stood and ruffled his hair the same way he'd messed with hers. "Go get your bowl and spoon."

"Mommy." Ronnie tugged on Cheryl's leg. "Mommy, me . . . me, too!"

She lifted him up into the high chair. "Fruit Loops coming right up." Cheryl kissed him on the cheek.

Not long after the boys finished eating, Eddie walked into the kitchen, fumbling with his tie. "Honey, can you help with this? I hate ties."

"Stand still." Cheryl quickly redid the knot. "Now, you look even more handsome." She kissed him on the lips, lingering for a moment.

"Stop, Mommy. That's yucky," Mitch squealed.

Ronnie echoed his brother. "Yucky."

Eddie chuckled. "Yeah, Mommy, stop that right now."

He winked at Mitch and then waved at Ronnie.

"Anyway, congratulations on your professorship at UT." He pulled Cheryl in close. "I'm so proud of you."

"Thank you. Look at you, a high school history teacher." She squeezed him tight and giggled. "No more junior high school kids!"

Eddie smiled. "I hope I'm ready."

"Don't forget you have to drop Mitch off at kindergarten."

"Come on, Mitch. Let's go to school." Eddie held his hand out for his son.

"Wait a minute, Daddy." Mitch ran toward his mother. "I love you." Mitch kissed her and hugged her close.

As Eddie watched Cheryl and the boys together, he knew that his family was what he lived for each day. It was why he came home. Eddie couldn't imagine his life without Cheryl, Mitch, and Ronnie. And the baby soon to come.

They strolled hand-in-hand out the front door.

FIRST DAY AT WORK

Once he'd dropped Mitch off at school, Eddie spent the dreary drive to work obsessing about the picture of the fishermen in Seadrift, Texas. The article wasn't favorable toward them because the locals resented the Vietnamese refugees for taking over their fishing waters.

He wondered how in the hell Dang got to the States in the first place, and how he'd then managed to move from Berkeley to Seadrift.

How did a murderer get into the country?

Eddie turned off the highway onto Cesar Chavez Street in the direction of Stephen F. Austin High School. When he pulled into the large parking lot, Eddie could see Town Lake close to the school building.

He believed Austin was a far better place than Berkeley to raise his boys. Although it was the capital of Texas, it still had a small-town feel and a close-knit community. Many of the residents were hippies, and its largest employers were the state government and the University of Texas.

When Cheryl was finally offered a teaching position at the university, they'd jumped at the opportunity, thinking the move would be a good thing for the family. Besides, Eddie hadn't cared for California that much.

However, he did miss his friend, Professor, the best man at Eddie's wedding and the one who'd served with him during his first tour in 'Nam along with Mitch Drexler.

After they'd moved, Eddie continued his training and workouts at the gym. He'd filled out the last couple of years and managed to put on twenty pounds of hard, lean muscle. He no longer had the teenage body he once did; now he sported the muscular physique of a fit thirty-year-old.

While at the gym, a workout buddy taught him taekwondo. Not that he became an expert, but it'd been enough to condition his body and mind and help him brush up on his self-defense.

His first day at Stephen F. Austin High School started like any other new job.

He met with the principal, assistant principal, and school secretary, all of whom confirmed that he had read the volumes of handbooks supplied to him about the school district rules.

Eddie—Mr. Henderson, to the pupils—loved talking with the students and was sure that the best part was sharing his passion for history. But he got disappointed and frustrated with himself if a student seemingly didn't have the same enthusiasm as he did.

At lunchtime, Eddie went to the library to research Vietnamese immigrants in the Houston area, using his break to pore over old newspaper articles and learn as much as he could about the refugees who had risked their lives to come to America.

America owed most of these people the freedom they sought.

When the last bell rang, Eddie left school swiftly to dash off and pick up Mitch and Ronnie from daycare.

Once home, the three of them played until Cheryl returned from work.

It was their routine—one he loved, one that was special.

•

While the boys played and Cheryl clattered about in the kitchen fixing dinner, Eddie slowly slipped into the bedroom and closed the door softly behind him. He waited a moment to see if Cheryl had followed him, wondering what he was doing.

The hallway was silent, so he pulled down a scuffed leather bag he kept tucked away on the top shelf of the closet.

It had been a long, long time since he'd touched this old traveling case, and he coughed as a cloud of gray dust loosened from its surface and cascaded down over his face.

The fine dust smelled of past times . . . and unfinished business.

After he opened the bag, he ran his fingers along the disassembled Winchester Model Seventy, and then delicately picked up the Weaver scope.

The last time he'd had the rifle assembled, he'd had the scope centered on Billy Matheson's forehead as he sat on the rooftop across the street from Billy's house, his finger on the trigger.

Before Mitch Drexler died, Eddie had held him momentarily in his arms and promised him he would kill Billy for taking his wife, Sandra. Yet he couldn't do it—he couldn't kill a man that wasn't attempting to kill him.

"Eddie, dinner's ready," Cheryl yelled from the kitchen.

"I'm coming."

He quickly zipped the bag and put it back in its hiding place.

I still need a pistol, something I can hide when I carry it.

Dinner time unfolded as usual: Eddie talking to the boys about their day, and them acting silly as they told him about their schoolwork or playtime. Cheryl hugged them both, showering them with love as she gave them more of their favorite food. It was a scene he savored every time.

Eddie glanced around the table and couldn't be happier.

After dinner, once the boys were in bed, Eddie shuffled up next to Cheryl on the sofa. His first thought was to light a cigarette.

But he didn't. He simply smiled, thankful that Cheryl's good-natured nagging had finally gotten him to quit several years ago.

He reached out his hand to gently rest on her belly. "He move at all today?"

He lovingly slid his hand across her stomach, caressing its roundness.

She leaned into him placing her hand on his. "Well, I'm only fifteen weeks, you know? And anyway, Ray wants to sleep most of the time. Says it's exhausting in there . . ."

Eddie smiled. "I sure hope his first words aren't gawddamn it."

They laughed together, long, loud, and heartily, knowing that had been Ray Laurel's favorite phrase. The thought united them.

Eddie and Laurel had served two tours in Vietnam together. Laurel had been younger, shorter, and skinnier than Eddie, and they'd been captured by the Viet Cong together. They'd been an inseparable pair. Buddies.

Eddie could still see Laurel's eyes and hear his pleading voice moments before Dang put a bullet through his skull.

Even if he never killed Dang in the end, at least he could name his son after Ray Laurel. That much he could do, and he'd see it done in a heartbeat.

And if his boy ever grew to be even a tenth of the man Laurel was, that was more than anyone could hope for.

He glanced at Cheryl, taking in her features—round, emerald-green eyes, perfectly spaced, with a small, upturned nose and full lips. When she smiled, dimples appeared.

Eddie stroked her long red hair. "I knew our children would have your hair."

Cheryl grinned. "Well, maybe little Ray will turn out to have brown hair, more like yours." She stood. "It's been a long day. I'm heading for bed. You coming?"

He let her pull him to his feet.

"You bet."

·

As he lay next to Cheryl, he knew that she stayed awake, waiting for the inevitable. He didn't know if his dreams that night would be about Ray Laurel or Mitch Drexler, or good times or bad times—or dreams somewhere between.

Eddie felt her finger trace along his spine as if to soothe him. He would be restless again soon, and she knew it. He fought sleep, too.

She lay there, waiting for his sleep to come, lying tense and anticipating. Same as always.

Her warm breath crawled along his skin each time she exhaled.

Eventually, he lost the battle and fell toward sleep, hoping he wouldn't hurt Cheryl inadvertently in the night—battling demons, chasing shadows, and seeking out revenge.

CHAPTER 4

THE BOAT PEOPLE

The next morning, Eddie arrived at school earlier than usual. After opening the classroom, he strode off in the direction of the library.

There was one thing on his mind.

He searched for older newspaper articles about the other Vietnamese immigrants who lived in Seadrift. The goal was to find a link between Dang and the fishermen, maybe something that identified him.

One article from the *Statesman* got his attention. There was another picture of Dang, and this newspaper clipping identified the man in the photograph as a union leader for the Vietnamese fishermen. Unfortunately, it didn't give his name, so Eddie decided that during his lunch break he would call the reporter who wrote the article.

He couldn't focus for the rest of the morning, and fidgeted like a kid with chickenpox. His body was filled with nervous anticipation— or maybe it was the excitement of finding Dang and getting the opportunity to avenge Ray. Eddie didn't know if he could get through the morning or even hold a conversation without his thoughts wandering off again.

After the noon bell rang, Eddie stopped by the cafeteria and picked up a roast beef sandwich. It was his regular lunch, and it helped brighten the day. Once he'd paid, he rushed toward the teacher's lounge, a million thoughts racing through his mind. He already imagined his fingers curled around the black telephone handset, the speaker to his ear, the questions he would ask.

In the lounge, however, both telephones were in use. Eddie felt annoyed. The two teachers jabbered on, seemingly about nothing important at all—nothing that couldn't have waited.

Eddie poured himself a cup of coffee and sat in one of the chairs, facing the first teacher as she talked.

If looks could kill, she'd have died there on the spot. But she was oblivious, caught up in some meaningless chit-chat about something or other.

Eddie noted that she was roughly ten years older than him, wearing a blue short-sleeved dress that hung several inches below her slim knees. Her graying hair was pulled back in a tight bun, perhaps a little harsh for her delicate features—the kind of austere hair that could make a woman frightening to a man.

But her voice was soft, and she laughed easily.

She sat with her back straight and knees pressed close together.

While glancing at Eddie, she shifted in her chair, holding the phone closer to her mouth so she could whisper. Within a couple of minutes, she returned the phone into its cradle. When the teacher finally stood, she shot Eddie a stern glance and left the lounge with quick short steps, not looking back. Evidently, his stares didn't go unnoticed.

Eddie rushed to the chair next to the vacant telephone and sat down, placing his lunch, coffee, pad, and pencil on the table.

For a moment, he hesitated—then gently removed the handset from the cradle. It was still warm from the woman's breath.

While he wolfed down the sandwich, Eddie dialed the reporter's number, smearing barbeque sauce on the buttons.

The phone rang three times.

"Hello, the *Statesman*. Jones speaking."

Eddie swallowed the bite of sandwich in his mouth, struggling to finish in time to speak. "Good afternoon, Mister Jones. I'm Eddie Henderson. I'm a history teacher at Austin High School."

"Hello, Mister Henderson. What can I do for you?"

"It's a little bit of a strange request, but I'm going to teach a class about the Boat People, and I have a question regarding an article you wrote this year. I'm hoping you can fill in a gap for me."

"Well, I'll try." Jones's voice turned serious. "Remind me first, which piece was that?"

"It's dated April twenty-third, nineteen-eighty. My question is about a man you referred to as a union leader."

"Hang on a minute. Let me see if I can find the article. I think I know the one you mean."

The line was quiet for several minutes. Eddie could hear the sound of rustling papers.

"Okay, I have it. And I've also found my notes about the interview."

Eddie tried to contain his excitement. *Stay calm,* he told himself. *Cool as a cucumber.*

"Well . . ." Eddie attempted to keep it from showing in his voice. "I don't suppose you have his full name and a possible address to get hold of him? I want to talk to him too."

"Well, I shouldn't really . . . You know how it goes. Confidentiality, data protection . . ." The reporter sounded hesitant.

"He'll want to hear from me." Eddie glanced around the room. "His story of leaving Vietnam after the war and coming to America will teach my students about perseverance and acceptance of other cultures. I believe he would enjoy sharing about his travels and how he built a new life in a strange country. This would be a real living history lesson. What a surprise for everyone! Don't you agree?"

His voice sounded weak. Maybe even a touch shaky. Was he credible?

He'd had to think off the top of his head. It was stupid not to have gone into the call with a story ready. *Screw this!*

Eddie felt sharply annoyed with himself. He couldn't get this close and then come up empty-handed.

He pressed his fingernails into his palms. It hurt.

"Hmm," the reporter's voice came again. "Well, I suppose I wouldn't have gotten this far without people telling me certain things they shouldn't, right?" The man laughed lightly.

Eddie could almost hear the cogs whirring in the journalist's brain.

He laughed too, attempting to keep it light and casual. "Right! I bet you've heard a few stories in your day!"

There was a short pause.

Then the other man spoke again.

"Okay, don't tell anyone it came from me. All I know is that his name is *Bảo Đặng*." He paused to spell out the words. "When I last spoke to him, he lived in the Little Saigon district in Houston. I don't have a residential address but . . . bear with me . . ."

He paused again for a moment, and the sound of rustling paper came back down the line.

"Yep, found it. His union office is in Little Saigon too. Again, no address, but it shouldn't be too hard to look him up."

Eddie dug his nails in his hand again, grinning.

"I hope that helps," the reporter said.

"Oh, it does. It does. Like I said, I believe he'll be delighted to hear from me. And it will be a big surprise."

Eddie's face lit up as he said his goodbye and slowly set the receiver back in its cradle. A wide smile spread across his face, the kind that hadn't appeared in many years.

He felt as if his insides would explode from the excitement, the success, and the sheer deviousness of it all. He'd had a good feeling about today even before he picked up the phone, believing he'd finally learn what he needed to know about Dang. Even though he hadn't been adequately prepared for the call, he was pleased with his unexpected ability to conjure up a storyline.

Eddie stood, holding back a shout of enthusiasm.

Lunchtime was over. Mission accomplished.

•

On the way back to the classroom the roast beef sandwich grumbled away in his excitable gut. But Eddie's mind was racing as he sorted through the new information and began to slot it in alongside all his research.

One thing Eddie had learned from his education was that knowledge could provide him with an advantage. Indeed, his mother had always said that if he paid attention to facts and was studious, it would pay off.

It seemed she'd been right.

Consequently, he had read everything he could get his hands on about the refugees from Vietnam, finding out that Texas held the second-highest number of Vietnamese immigrants after California.

And Eddie knew a great deal about the Vietnamese people who had fled after the fall of Saigon in 1975. Over the last five years, nearly a million refugees had made their way to America, many using small fishing boats or old cargo ships to cross the Pacific Ocean despite the many dangers. The name "boat people" was derived from these ocean crossings.

Immediately after the fall of Saigon, over 130,000 Vietnamese had settled in the States, and as a result, Houston now had one of the largest immigrant populations in Texas. Some Vietnamese refugees, the articles had said, had settled in the coastal town of Seadrift, 150 miles south of Houston.

They had a shaky start, but not just because of leftover prejudice from the war. The Vietnamese were enterprising competition for the prime fishing waters. Many of the local white fishermen resented the immigrants and openly showed their hostility.

Eddie wondered how the hell—despite all the clues he had now amassed—he could find Dang. There was such a large settlement of Vietnamese, and he knew they had large, extended families that all seemed to interlink, one into the next. And besides all that, he still had a tough time picturing the Viet Cong lieutenant as a fisherman.

I'm sure he is up to something no good. Sea-fishing, my ass!

However, his first mission needed to be recon to determine if Dang was even in the area. That first foray wouldn't be about making contact with him.

Slowly, slowly, that's the way to do it. He would focus on gathering information about Little Saigon and the Vietnamese people who inhabited the district. And he believed this could be a handy opportunity to take Cheryl on a trip away from Austin for a day.

Let's call it a day out, he told himself, smiling. *An away day!*

Houston had never before seemed so tempting.

But he'd have to be sure Cheryl didn't work out what their little road trip was all about.

TIME TO TELL HER

One week later, while sitting with Cheryl on a Friday evening, Eddie grinned, turned to her and asked, "Want to go to Houston tomorrow?"

She faced him. Her look was one of confusion.

"Houston? Why on earth would you want to go to Houston?"

"I want to see what the Vietnamese community is like." Eddie sat straighter. "It's not that far away, a little over a two-hour drive. Don't know . . . I fancy a trip, that's all."

Cheryl rolled her eyes. "Hmm, you sure it has nothing to do with that Lieutenant Dang?" She leaned forward. "And don't you lie to me either, Mister Eddie Henderson. I can always tell when you're lying. It's one skill you don't have."

"Well, maybe I'm a little curious about Dang." Eddie flashed his boyish grin. "I want to check the area out to see if he still works or lives there. But believe me, I'm not going to confront him." He took her hand. "I wouldn't do anything that would get you hurt. You know that."

Cheryl hesitated while she stared into his eyes.

She shrugged. "Okay, I'll go with you. Let's get the sitter to watch the boys. A day trip, right? And no funny business, if you know what I mean."

"Yep, a day trip. And I'll be good, promise." Eddie stood and pulled her to her feet. "I love you."

Cheryl smiled. "Me too. I mean, I love you too. I'll call the babysitter, and you make sure the car is ready for the trip, cold drinks packed and all. I'm taking it easy since you're treating me to time away from home."

She giggled as she walked away, muttering "Houston!" under her breath. Her shoulders shook from laughing.

Eddie grabbed his keys and wallet.

"That's a deal!" Eddie followed her into the kitchen and kissed her goodbye. "I'm leaving now to get gas, cold drinks, some munchies and a whole lot more."

•

As he walked to the blue four-door Ford Fairmont, an even bigger smile tugged at his lips. This sure was all going according to plan.

He drove roughly two miles on the main road before he turned into a large, well-spaced parking lot. He glanced at the sign over the doorway that read *Gun Shop*. Once he'd steered the car into a parking spot, he went inside the store.

Eddie walked directly toward the counter.

"Can I help you?" an older man asked. A gray mustache covered his upper lip and he wore a white, sweat-stained cowboy hat.

Eddie glanced at the showcase under the counter. "I want a military Colt forty-five-caliber pistol." He decided to buy a weapon that he was familiar with—he had qualified with the .45 while in the army.

Plus, he wanted a gun small enough to carry on him. The Winchester rifle was too large to carry around.

The clerk bent down and pulled out a pistol from the case. "How about this one? Just bought it. It's in brand-new condition."

Eddie took the weapon, making sure he pointed the gun away from anyone while keeping his finger out of the trigger housing.

He checked to see if a magazine was in the pistol, and then pulled the slide back, locking it in place.

After a quick inspection, Eddie handed the gun to the clerk. "I'll take it. Plus two loaded magazines." He glanced around the store.

The clerk looked surprised. "Don't you want to test fire it?" He lit a cigarette, casually blowing the smoke toward Eddie.

He waved his hand to move the flow of smoke away from him.

"Not today, maybe later. Ring up the sale, please."

Eddie reached into his back pocket and pulled out a wallet.

Once he'd paid, the clerk dropped the pistol and magazines into a bag. "There you go, son." He handed it to Eddie as he blew another mouthful of smoke his way.

Eddie turned sideways, screwing up his eyes. He coughed.

It was easier to get the hell out than argue over smoke. And besides, he had things to do.

"Thank you."

After he got back to the car, Eddie inserted a magazine into the pistol and hid it under the driver's seat, shoving it as far back as he could while still being able to reach it. Then he pushed the extra magazine under some car paperwork and McDonald's kids' meal toys in the glove box.

Next, Eddie climbed into the back seat and attempted to grab the gun by reaching from behind under the driver's seat. He smiled, able to confirm that the seat bar blocked the hiding spot, and there was no way his boys could get to the weapon.

On the way home, he stopped at the Seven-Eleven to gas up. After filling the gas tank, he went inside the store.

He selected some snacks for the trip and then paid the clerk.

Shopping expedition completed, it was time to head back home.

•

As he pulled into the driveway of their white stone three-bedroom, two-bath home, he felt guilt take hold. *It's for our protection,* he told himself, though not convincingly. Cheryl would go crazy if she knew what was lurking under the goddamn car seat.

Looks like it was his job to make sure she didn't find out.

When he opened the front door, Cheryl yelled from the kitchen, "The babysitter will be here at nine, is that okay?"

He placed the bag of snacks on the table and approached her as she stood with the refrigerator door open.

"Sure, nine is perfect. I got gas and snacks." He embraced her while nuzzling her neck. "Mmm. You smell so good."

She felt good too in her silky sleepwear.

Cheryl turned to face him. "And I'm ready for bed, how about you?"

"I am too." Eddie smiled and kissed her lightly on the lips. "Big day tomorrow. And anyway, I'm always ready for bed when you smell like that." He almost told Cheryl about the pistol because it was nagging at him, but he changed his mind.

He hated to deceive her, though. Eddie knew that they might need the protection if, by chance, they ran into Dang—but otherwise, he was attempting not to turn the gun into an essential part of tomorrow's mission.

He would leave it concealed and untouched if there was no threat to them. And then no harm would have been done, and no one would be the wiser. The only person who'd know was him.

In a perfect world, he'd share the news with Cheryl, but knew he'd only end up handing it over if he told her. And he was certainly not about to do that . . .

He was positive Cheryl would never understand how dangerous and cruel Dang was—that he would hurt Cheryl without hesitating for even a single second.

And maybe Dang would do more than simply hurt her.

Eddie shuddered, a cold shiver that traced its way right from the base of his skull to the bottom of his spine. If Dang were to do anything to Cheryl or the kids . . .

As he lay with his back to her in bed later that night, she stroked his shoulder with the tips of her fingers. Eddie didn't flinch like he usually did—now, he found her touch oddly calming. She was there, and they were safe, and that was all that mattered. Besides, he had a plan.

That made all the difference to his peace of mind.

So he believed.

His eyes stared at the wall that he couldn't see anyway, the room shrouded in inky blackness—but he did it as a means to focus his mind. He again considered his actions and how they might affect her and, potentially, baby Ray and their other kids.

He suddenly rolled over and snuggled extra close to Cheryl with his arms around her. His eyes were misty.

Thankfully, she couldn't have known there was a tear falling down his cheek because of the blackness between them, but he wiped his eyes with the back of one hand, stifling the urge to sniffle.

"I love you." Cheryl closed her eyes.

Eddie snored softly in no time, though his mind was not as peaceful as things may have appeared. Cheryl's presence could lull him into a gentle sleep, but it could never put an end to his horrendous nightmares.

•

From a deep sleep, Eddie bolted upright in bed. "Mitch, I'm coming, hold on! Hold on, buddy!" He flipped to his side, falling to the floor. "Where's my rifle? I can't find my fucking rifle!"

Cheryl instantaneously and silently slid out of bed, her silk nightgown almost constructed for the job of allowing her a single, sleek movement down to the bedroom carpet, barely even disturbing the bedding as she went. This routine was becoming second nature to her, a well-rehearsed action, something she knew how to do almost without thinking. She could probably even do it in her sleep—but fortunately, of the two of them, she was the one who always woke at every little thing. Every cough, every unusual shift in the bed, every small word uttered in Eddie's confusion, and she was wide awake.

These days, she even awoke if a small bird perched on the sill outside, or if the wind blowing through the trees rattled a second too long. Eddie's nervousness was teaching her to be on edge.

Now, she sat on the floor in front of him, as always, hugging her knees, as she had done many times over the years.

She always longed to reach out and hug him to her, but she never did, not until he was ready. She was afraid of what he might do if he mistook her for someone else.

"Eddie, it's okay. It's me, Cheryl. You'll be okay. Shh . . ."

He jerked away. "Help Mitch!"

She took his hands into hers.

"Eddie, you're home. You're safe. It's me, Cheryl."

He sat upright, looking around the room, beads of glistening sweat dripping down his face. His pounding heart pushed blood through his veins until he thought they would explode.

She cradled him in her arms, safe to do so now that he was awake.

"It's okay. It's okay." She rocked him softly.

He gasped. "Shit. I'm sorry, Cheryl." He pulled away. "I can't believe I'm still having these dreams."

Cheryl touched his arm while looking at the clock. "Well, it's five o'clock. We might as well get up and have breakfast before the boys are up and about."

Eddie wiped the sweat from his brow.

"I'm sorry. I'll get the coffee going."

ROAD TRIP TO LITTLE SAIGON

Not long after they were ready for the trip, the doorbell rang. Cheryl set her cup on the counter. "I'll get it. It's probably the neighbor." Mrs. Dalton was coming over to watch the boys. She bolted through the living room as if her life depended on it, never one to keep a person waiting.

As Cheryl opened the door, Mrs. Dalton said, "Good morning. I hope I'm not too early." She was middle-aged with a still-youthful figure and a pleasant smile, but was otherwise plain. Some may have called her maternal-looking—or simply boring.

The two women seemed poles apart, but they had become firm friends not long after Cheryl, Eddie and the boys moved in.

Cheryl smiled and waved her inside. "Not at all, right on time."

Once they said their goodbyes to the boys, they were on the road in no time, driving to Houston. Eddie didn't have a plan. For him, this was a reconnaissance mission more than anything else. He glanced at Cheryl and had second thoughts about bringing her with him.

So, what if we do run into Dang, then what?

As he drove along the highway, he placed a hand on his wife's rounded stomach. "How's my little Ray doing this morning?"

Cheryl beamed. She visibly loved it whenever he asked.

"He's making his presence felt, like his dad always did, trying to win my attention. And he's getting more active and sleeping less, thumping away at my belly with his fists, making sure I get no rest. Again, a bit like you, what with our early morning awakenings and all that."

They both laughed, though the frequent nightmares were more of a problem than either liked to admit.

Cheryl gazed fondly at her husband as he drove.

"Anyway, what did you learn about the refugees?" she inquired.

"I didn't think you would ever ask." Eddie smiled and sat straighter in his seat. "Did you know that the first refugees from Vietnam were mainly politicians, military officers, and other highly educated professionals?"

Cheryl giggled. "No, I didn't know that. My, you have been doing your homework Mister Eddie Henderson, you may go to the top of the class and get yourself a gold star!"

They laughed again. But he had yet more to tell.

"And I also found out that most of them spoke English well. I think we got some of the country's best minds after Saigon fell."

Eddie grinned at his wife.

"Well, that's good to know." Cheryl put her hand over Eddie's as he gently rubbed her stomach with his right hand.

Eddie glanced at Cheryl, looking to see her expression as he related what he learned. He was pleased to see she looked interested.

"Because you're so keen to know, here's another tidbit of information. The groups of refugees that followed had less education and fewer resources than the earlier, educated group. Few of them spoke English."

"So, are they doing as well as the earlier groups?"

"Not as good, but they are blending into society and doing better than they would back in 'Nam under the Communists." Eddie removed his hand from Cheryl's stomach and grasped the steering wheel as they curved around a gentle bend. "But let's not forget about people like Dang who came to America to exploit their own people and hook up with soldiers they served with back in Vietnam."

Cheryl remained silent now, staring out the window.

Once they were closer to Houston, she took hold of the map and spread it out on her lap, giving directions to get to Little Saigon.

"Turn here. That's Bellaire Boulevard. That should lead us to the Vietnamese neighborhoods." Cheryl pointed to her right.

Eddie turned onto Bellaire Boulevard, driving down the main street into the district known as Little Saigon. He saw some street signs in Vietnamese. Restaurants and small shops lined the boulevard, with shoppers strolling along the crowded sidewalks.

He pointed at a flag fluttering in the breeze in front of a restaurant. "Cheryl, look at that, a South Vietnamese flag." Eddie pulled into a parking spot in front of the building. "This is as good a place to start as any."

Cheryl looked at the sign in the window.

"What are pho noodles?" she asked.

"It's a Vietnamese soup that's a broth with rice noodles, herbs, and meat. Usually beef but sometimes chicken. Pho is probably the most famous Vietnamese dish." Eddie scanned the area.

"I want to try it." Cheryl giggled. "Just to say I had it."

"Well, it's almost lunchtime. You know, this is what Mitch and I had in that small village. Mama-san made it for us. Vinh kept on repeating the sound of a dog barking to tell us what meat was in it."

He searched her eyes for a reaction.

Cheryl's face scrunched up, and then she smiled. "I still want some."

"I always believed you were brave." He grinned as he gazed into her eyes. "Game for anything."

She laughed. "Not quite anything."

He nodded silently, acknowledging his promise to cause no trouble.

When he stepped out of the car, the smells of Little Saigon hit him with full force. And it wasn't only the smells, either; it was the people, the shops, and the activity going on around him that sent him to the past. Every small thing seemed to act as a trigger.

A thousand images of his time in Vietnam flashed through his mind like a movie on fast forward. Even the danger warning signals made his body react as if the VC were approaching.

While Cheryl's back was to him, he reached under the seat and grabbed the pistol. In one swift motion, he tucked it into his waistband, then covered the gun with his T-shirt. He hoped she wouldn't notice.

When they approached the restaurant, he looked at his reflection to see if a bulge showed. Eddie smiled; he didn't notice, so she wouldn't either.

From their seat right by the large plate glass window, Eddie observed the locals coming and going. An older woman shuffled over to their table. She smiled, showing her blackened teeth, no doubt the effect from many years of chewing betel nut. She had her gray hair pulled back into a stark bun, reminding Eddie of the schoolteacher who'd made him wait for the use of the phone the day he had called the reporter.

This woman wore the traditional black silk shirt and pants with sandals. Eddie believed she could've walked right from a Vietnamese village into the streets of Houston, as if she had teleported there.

"*Bạn muốn gì?*" *What do you want?*

She held a pencil and pad and pointed at the menu.

Eddie held up two fingers. "Two pho noodles and two *cà phê đá.*"

The waitress nodded, smiled her gapped smile, and slowly shuffled toward the rear of the restaurant as if afraid she might topple over if the soles of her sandals lost contact with the carpet.

Cheryl put her hand on Eddie's.

"Wow! I didn't know you could speak Vietnamese. How can I have been with you all this time and not known that!"

Eddie laughed. "That's about all I do know. So don't get too excited. And besides, you have no idea if what I said was correct."

Cheryl gave him a sideways glance.

"We'll soon get to find out. What did you order besides the pho?"

"Ice coffee, another Vietnamese favorite." Eddie placed his other hand over hers. "You'll like it."

"This restaurant looks, I don't know—quaint." Cheryl glanced around the small room with a handful of tables.

Eddie smiled. "You'll probably find most businesses around here look like this. Owned and operated by a family."

The old woman returned, setting down two Vietnamese ice coffees.

Eddie pulled out the newspaper article. "Do you know this man?" He pointed at Dang in the picture.

She smiled while shaking her head, no.

"*Cảm ơn bạn.*" *Thank you.* Eddie slightly lowered his head.

After the woman headed for the kitchen, a little girl brought the two bowls of noodles. "I hope you enjoy our pho." She set them on the table.

Cheryl turned in her chair. "Thank you. I'm sure we will." She reached out and touched the girl's arm. "How old are you?"

The girl with long black hair, wearing a multi-colored dress with sneakers, giggled. "I'm eight."

Eddie took the opportunity to show the photograph to the little girl. First, she looked around the restaurant, then shook her head no that she didn't know the men. She scampered back to the kitchen, laughing.

They sat silently, eating the meal. Eddie put his spoon down and smiled at Cheryl. He picked up the bowl, tilted it to his lips, and finished off the pho with a loud slurp.

"What are you doing?" Cheryl's face flushed as she looked around the room. "You're slurping your soup."

"You have to slurp. It's polite." He burped. "And that's how you finish the meal. Shows you're satisfied. You know, it shows that the hostess gave you enough good food to eat."

Cheryl's eyebrows rose. "Well, I'm not going to manage to do it."

"You can slurp a little, can't you?"

"But I can't burp. Not even in the interest of politeness."

He laughed. "I think they'll forgive you. Possibly."

She picked up her bowl and drank the soup.

After the last drop slid down her throat, she set the bowl on the table and wiped her lips with the napkin. There had not been a single slurp.

Eddie gave a mischievous smile. "So, you're not going to burp?"

Cheryl let loose a long, loud burp.

It was unexpected, but sounded satisfying. "Oh, my God, really, I did not expect that. Pardon me!" She appeared embarrassed now, and Eddie's shoulders shook with laughter.

"See, good and satisfying soup!" Eddie chuckled.

"Shh!"

The other customers kept on eating and talking as if they hadn't heard a sound, to Cheryl's relief.

"Now that's my Cheryl." Eddie let out a loud belly laugh.

After the meal, they spent the afternoon walking along the sidewalk, talking and laughing. She made Eddie go into the many different shops.

At every opportunity, he pulled out the picture, asking the same question about Dang. Each time, Eddie received a negative response.

At one shop, Cheryl eyed a delicate yellow-and-pink paper kite. She ran her finger along the edges. "You can fly these with the boys at Zilker Park. Should I buy some?"

"Great idea. That would be fun."

Eddie scanned the many shelves that held the kites. "You pick out what you like—too many for me to choose from."

After Cheryl paid for two kites, she rubbed her stomach.

"I think we can safely say I'm tired. Let's go home. You don't mind, do you?" she asked.

"You're not feeling unwell or anything?"

She giggled. "No. Just sleepy. The soup went to my head."

"Okay. So I got you drunk on soup. Home it is, then."

Eddie grabbed her hand protectively as they approached the curb and started walking back toward the car parked about a block down the boulevard. As they approached the vehicle, he observed three men standing on the corner near the front of the restaurant where they'd had lunch, talking and smoking.

They were similarly attired, wearing slacks with a sports jacket, and each one had short dark hair. They stood tall with their shoulders back while they glanced around as they talked.

People strolling along the sidewalk made a point to walk around the men, giving them plenty of room, and no one seemed happy to make eye contact. There was something about them that seemed out of place; they appeared more like soldiers than residents casually hanging out on the street corner.

They were shifty, emanating an uneasiness that set the locals on edge like a bird of prey among sparrows. People scuttled by, eager to pass.

Even odder, Eddie observed a man standing near his car taking pictures. When they approached with car keys in hand, Eddie noticed the Vietnamese man's right eye twitched while his mouth held onto a harsh scowl. Most notably were the acne scars that covered his face. The man acted nervous and strode away swiftly in the opposite direction, silent, skulking off like a rat caught in a grain barrel.

"What was that about?" Cheryl asked.

Eddie surveyed the street. "I'm not sure."

He removed the newspaper clipping from his pocket. "Go ahead and get in the car. I'm going to ask those guys." He opened the passenger door for her. "Last time, I promise."

When he approached the group, the talking stopped.

They stood straighter now, feet apart, fists clenched. Eddie felt uncomfortable—and he sensed danger. His instincts told him to turn around and go back to the car and act as if he hadn't seen them, the same way everyone else appeared to. People seemed accustomed to pretending these men were invisible.

He didn't listen to his gut and stopped in front of the group.

Eddie flashed his boyish grin.

"Good afternoon. I am sorry to interrupt, but I was wondering, do you happen to know this man?"

The three men stared at Eddie. After a long ten to fifteen seconds, the biggest man in the group roughly snatched the clipping from Eddie's hands. He looked at the photograph and then he showed it to his friends. All the while, they spoke to each other in Vietnamese, ignoring Eddie. He glanced at each face not understanding a word they said.

There was the slightest tell from the man who was looking at the newspaper article. Maybe it was the way he glanced at Eddie's car after looking at the photograph. Before, Eddie wasn't sure why the man was interested in his car, but it was at this moment that he knew—for certain—that Dang was onto his questions.

The man handed Eddie the photo. "No. Don't know him."

"Please look again." This time he pointed at Dang. "This one, see."

The three men turned as one and strode away.

Again, he sensed that something wasn't right. He got the impression that they might have lied to him. The three men knew Dang; he could feel it, sense it. Dang must have been somewhere close by, maybe watching, holding Eddie firmly in his sights while he stood on the corner.

Eddie tilted his head back and looked around, searching for Dang's face. His nose wrinkled, and for a moment, the color drained from his face as if he had seen a ghost.

He *knew* someone was watching him.

Although fear gripped him, Eddie took the index finger of his right hand and slowly traced it from the corner of his right eye to his lower jaw. Then he smiled. *How about that then, motherfucker?*

When he got into the car, Cheryl asked, "What was that about?"

"I suspect those three guys know Dang. He's nearby right now, I can feel it." Eddie started the car.

He removed the pistol from his waistband and slid it under the seat.

"My God, Eddie. What are you doing?" Cheryl gasped.

"I'm protecting my family. You don't know how dangerous these men are. Dang would kill you, the boys, and me without even hesitating. You need to trust me on this, Cheryl."

"I don't have a choice, do I?" She turned in her seat and stared out the window. "If he's as dangerous as you're saying, maybe revenge isn't the answer." She sighed, unable to believe what she'd seen Eddie do with her own eyes.

He could tell that Cheryl felt as if he had broken his promise to her. And he had.

On the ride home they sat in silence. He glanced at Cheryl as she persisted in sitting at an awkward angle, her body turned away from him toward the side window.

"You need to turn around, Cheryl. Look, the seatbelt's digging into your belly. It can't be good for baby Ray."

"I'm perfectly fine." She stared out the window. "And Ray's fine."

"Do it for me then. I'm worried about you sitting like that."

"Me sitting sideways should be the least of your worries." The look she shot him radiated anger. "Carrying a handgun and going around asking questions isn't exactly looking after me. And you promised . . ."

She turned away again, and he could swear her voice faltered.

"It's for your protection. You know it is," he answered.

"And if you didn't ask questions where you shouldn't, and if you didn't go around with hidden weapons, maybe I wouldn't need protecting."

Eddie knew she was rightly pissed at his need to discover Dang's whereabouts, and for buying a pistol and putting the whole family in what was sure to be a precarious position.

But, on the other hand, if she knew the full extent of Dang's cruelty, what he'd done to him and Ray, she would bless his obsession to find him.

Eddie, buried in his thoughts, had to figure out how he would stop Dang. No . . . how he would kill him. Because now, by his own admission, he feared for his family. He had put them directly in harm's way, even if they hadn't been there already. He was beginning to hate himself.

HATRED WAS ALL THEY HAD

Once home from the Houston trip, the days turned into weeks as Eddie and Cheryl went about their daily activities.

Neither spoke of Dang.

Eddie's hatred consumed him, and the need to kill Dang grew stronger every day. The desire for revenge relentlessly gnawed at him as if something in his guts wanted out. He'd promised Ray Laurel. Eddie didn't care how it happened—he wanted the life in Dang's cold black eyes snuffed out forever.

Eddie felt certain Dang knew he had found him in Little Saigon, and he wondered who would be the first to confront the other. *Revenge is coming. It's coming real soon.*

His mind incessantly whirled with scenarios of possible ways to kill Dang, eliminating those with obvious flaws. It wasn't like he could track him down in the jungles of Vietnam and kill him with no one the wiser. Hell, no one would care.

In the States, it would be considered murder, regardless of Dang's crimes during the war. He had no desire to go to prison and leave his family, but he wouldn't play by "the rules" either. The plan had to be perfect.

•

Meanwhile, in the weeks since Dang had seen Eddie in Little Saigon, he'd made plans of his own. He wanted revenge as much as Eddie did. The obvious crossed Dang's mind—he should've killed him after he shot Ray Laurel. If he had, he wouldn't have this problem today.

He remembered the rage he felt when he saw Eddie talking to three of his men on that corner in Little Saigon. He could feel it starting to boil again thinking about Eddie searching for him. The hatred made his body shake so much it surprised him.

How could he ever forget that Eddie slashed his face before the American soldiers captured him and then sent him to the prisoner-of-war compound in Chu Lai? The ugly scar reminded him every day.

He regretted not killing Eddie before moving to Houston. The opportunity had presented itself while he was living in Berkeley. When downtown one evening, he'd spotted Eddie at a restaurant, but decided to let it wait for another time. Taunting him and his pretty wife did give Dang a small amount of pleasure.

Now that he'd given his contacts at the Department of Motor Vehicles Eddie's license plate number, Dang knew exactly where he lived in Austin. He'd dispatched *Cánh* and *Nguyễn* there with instructions to follow Eddie and learn his routine. They were to stay out of sight and report back on what they observed. He didn't want his underlings interacting with Eddie—he wanted the first contact himself.

Dang planned to strike first, and without warning. He wanted to terrorize Eddie and his family before he killed him. Dang removed a photograph from his shirt pocket and stared at it for several moments. His thin, cruel smile grew while he gazed at the image of Cheryl.

CHAPTER 8

AN OLD FRIEND

After about a month of teaching high school, Eddie was starting to feel comfortable in the classroom. There were roughly nineteen students in each of his classes, and he was becoming familiar with each one.

One day, before the first-period bell rang, the principal entered Eddie's room. "Mr. Henderson, you have a minute?" he asked.

Eddie looked up from his morning paper. "Sure, what do you need?"

"You're getting a new student Monday of next week. He'll be in your homeroom and first-period history class." He stood a little straighter. "I understand you're a Vietnam veteran. Is that right?"

"Yes, that's correct." Eddie stood and rubbed his jaw. "Is that a problem?"

The principal smiled. "Oh, no, not at all. It's that the new student is Vietnamese, and I figured you might work better with him." He paused and wiped his glasses. "With you having been in Vietnam and all." After a slight hesitation he continued. "He scored better than average on the tests and speaks English well, but he's still heavily accented."

Eddie smiled. "You do know I don't speak Vietnamese?"

The principal picked at lint on his jacket. "I know, but I thought you might have a better understanding of the culture than most teachers. And as I say, he understands English more than adequately."

"Sure, I'll be happy to have the new student."

"Thank you. And by the way, I've heard nothing but good things about you." He turned and strode out of the classroom.

Eddie knew there were about two thousand Vietnamese refugees in Austin, many of whom received sponsorship from the Westlake Hills Presbyterian Church. After he'd thought for a moment, he smiled, thinking it odd that a Presbyterian would take in a Buddhist.

He recalled that most of the villagers he'd had contact with in Vietnam were Buddhist, but he had heard a lot of the Vietnamese living in the cities were Catholics.

Whatever religion someone holds dear didn't matter to Eddie— God left him when he was in Vietnam.

•

On Monday morning, Eddie got to school a little earlier than usual. There was an odd fluttering in his gut, which he attributed to the fact that the new student was joining him today. A shared Vietnamese history—as limited as it was—could certainly make things a little more interesting. Plus, it was a privilege to have been chosen for the task.

It seemed someone had noticed his good work. Eddie was going places.

So, after the morning ritual of filling his coffee cup, he went off to the classroom with a spring in his step for a change.

The classroom had one large window that let in the sunlight, and the room held twenty individual school desks, one for each student. His sizeable wooden office desk faced the students, with the blackboard behind him.

He thought the desk was from the forties, and it had many scratches that he believed gave it additional character.

The off-white tiled floor shone from being recently polished.

It was starting as a mighty fine day indeed—the sun shining, the coffee made to perfection, and the schoolroom gleaming as he liked it.

Plus, he had a little time to spare before class.

He sat in the matching wooden chair, swung his feet onto the desktop, and began reading the newspaper with the sun warming his back.

"Good morning."

A soft voice echoed in the empty room.

Startled, Eddie lowered the paper while whipping his feet down from the desk and standing.

"Good morning, I'm Mr. Henderson." He extended his hand.

Although the boy had already spoken two words of a perfectly fine greeting, it now seemed that he couldn't talk all of a sudden. The boy didn't return Eddie's greeting, and a strange sense of tension filled the air between the two.

The now wary-looking Vietnamese student stood with his mouth open, staring at his new teacher as if beholding a mirage. It seemed that the boy wanted to say more, but Eddie only heard heavy breathing and a couple of indecipherable grunts.

To make matters worse, tears welled in the student's eyes.

Eddie didn't know what to do. "Are you okay? Do you want me to call someone?" He reached out and placed a hand on the student's shoulder.

The boy gasped. "Eddie."

Now it was Eddie's mouth that hung open. He stared at the student, no older than eighteen, and yet there was something familiar about him.

He couldn't breathe. "Vinh?"

"Yes, it's me." Vinh fell into Eddie's arms.

Eddie held him by the shoulders. "Well, I never! Look at you, all grown up. You're a man now." He hugged him.

When he'd last seen Vinh, the boy had been Dang's prisoner.

The Viet Cong had shown up at the village, abruptly taking young Vinh and forcing him to help them. Despite being a traumatized young boy, it had been Vinh who'd helped Eddie rather than the other way around.

Vinh had brought him food and water and comforted him one day during captivity. And it had been Vinh who had risked his own life to give Eddie his boots, untying him and allowing him to escape.

"I see you two have met."

The principal stood in the doorway with his chin raised and lips pressed together. "Mr. Henderson, please see me before school starts."

"Sure, no problem. I'll be right there."

He spoke to the principal, but his gaze stayed firmly transfixed upon his friend's face. It was surreal to see the boy right here before him, in Austin, Texas, of all places.

Vinh stepped away from Eddie. "I'm sorry. I didn't mean to cause you trouble."

"Vinh, it's okay. Look, take the last desk in the third row." Eddie pointed across the classroom to the usually vacant desk. He adjusted his tie then pushed his fingers through his hair.

"We have a lot of catching up to do."

Eddie left the classroom, heading toward the principal's office.

On arrival, he peered in the doorway. "You wanted to see me?"

"Yes, come in." The principal stood behind his desk. "You do know that we don't hug our students, don't you?"

Eddie smiled. "I do. But Vinh and I go way back. We know each other." He moved inside the doorway and stood with feet apart and hands on hips. "That boy saved my life."

"I didn't know . . ." The principal sat in his chair. "But nevertheless, please don't hug the students." He arranged the pens on his desk. "That information was in the district rulebook."

Eddie clenched his fists. "Got it. Anything else?"

"No, and thank you for stopping by my office."

Eddie turned on his heels, going toward the classroom with an ear-to-ear smile on his face. He didn't care what the principal had to say about his interaction with Vinh. It was fate that had brought them back together, and he had no intention of losing him again.

And besides, petty rules were made to be ignored in situations such as this.

Once back in the classroom, the students went quiet.

Eddie called Vinh to his desk. "After the last bell, would you stop by here? Can you come to dinner tonight?"

Vinh smiled. "Yes, I would like that."

"Great, I'll call Cheryl later and tell her. Let me introduce you." Eddie walked to the front of the desk. "Good morning, class. We have a new student for homeroom and first period. His name is Vinh, and he's come to us all the way from the Quang Ngai Province in Vietnam."

Eddie stood straighter, squaring his shoulders. "And I think we can all agree he's an American now. So please make him feel welcome."

•

After the last bell rang, Vinh strolled into the classroom, his eyes shining and filled with eagerness. Eddie observed the teenager with his shock of black hair, thin muscular build, and friendly face. His smile showed full rows of even, white teeth, slightly too big for his mouth, as if his face had not quite grown to fit them. But Eddie couldn't believe how much the rest of Vinh had developed. He was almost taller than him now.

No longer was he the little boy Eddie once knew.

Vinh stopped at the desk. "Hello, Mr. Henderson. I'm ready."

Eddie stood. "Do you need me to call anyone to let them know that you're going with me?"

"No, there's no one." Vinh's smile disappeared.

"Oh, okay. Well, now you have Cheryl and me. You'll like my wife." Eddie headed for the door with Vinh following.

On the trip home, they stopped at the daycare and picked up the boys. Once Eddie got the two boys buckled into the back seat, he climbed behind the wheel.

As soon as Eddie sat down, Mitch asked, "Daddy, who is that man?"

"Daddy, who is he?" Ronnie echoed.

Eddie turned around in his seat. "Mitch and Ronnie, this is an old friend of mine. His name is Vinh."

Mitch laughed. "That's a funny name."

Vinh turned in his seat too, beginning to ask questions about the cartoon, *The Flintstone Comedy Show*. Now he had their attention. It seemed Vinh knew how to speak to children in their language.

His peculiar accent didn't even get in the way.

Vinh looked at Eddie. "I learned a lot of English from cartoons." Vinh turned his attention to the two boys. "Yabba dabba doo!"

They giggled and said in unison, "Yabba dabba doo!"

"Daddy, I like Vinh." Mitch squirmed in his seat attempting to lean forward.

Ronnie echoed, "Me too, Daddy. Is Vinh coming to stay with us, Daddy? Is he, Daddy? Can he?"

Eddie laughed, his whole face splitting into a wide grin.

"He's only joining us for dinner, boys, so be on your best behavior. But if you don't scare him off, maybe Vinh will come again."

When Eddie opened the front door of his home, he could smell the aroma of pot roast. He smiled again, knowing that there would be a lemon pound cake too. Cheryl knew how to spoil them all.

The boys ran to Cheryl, yelling, "Mommy, Mommy."

Each one grabbed a leg and wouldn't let go.

After he closed the door, Eddie said, "Cheryl, this is Vinh."

Cheryl had to pull the boys off so she could walk. "Welcome, Vinh." She raced toward the startled teenager and embraced him. "Thank you for saving Eddie. Thank you," she cried. "Oh, thank you."

"Okay, Cheryl. You can let go now." Eddie tugged on her arm. "Let the boy breathe."

She stepped back, wiping away tears.

"Well, I hope you like pot roast as much as Eddie."

"Yes, I do. I love roast dinner." Vinh licked his lips.

"Good, we have plenty."

Cheryl went into the kitchen with the boys following.

•

After dinner, Eddie and Vinh remained at the table talking while Cheryl got the boys ready for bed. Eddie began clearing the table and cleaning dishes while they spoke.

Vinh leaped from his chair and went to grab some of the plates from Eddie's hands. "Please, I help you clear up."

"No, no, no. You're my guest. Our guest! And what a special guest you are to me. So, I'm afraid there'll be no chores for you. But there is one thing you could do for me, if you like."

"What is that?" Vinh asked, eager to know what his task was.

"It's simple. I would love for you to tell me what happened after you helped me escape." Eddie asked. "How did things go for you after that? It must've been . . . terrible."

Vinh squirmed in his seat. "I will tell you, but you know, it is not easy. Give me a moment, please."

He took a deep breath and his eyes watered.

Eddie leaned forward, resting a hand on Vinh's forearm.

"Look, I'm sorry. Forget that I asked. It was stupid of me."

"No, I will tell you." Vinh's voice got louder. He had now psyched himself up to tell the tale. "So . . . well, Lieutenant Dang was so angry at two of his soldiers, thinking they helped you escape. After asking them many questions and beating them with sticks, he finally said they would die. And I can remember the boy—he had big tears rolling down his face from the fear, you know? And I remember him saying to Dang, *oh, no don't* . . ." He looked out the window. "And so the two soldiers kneeled on the ground facing the jungle. And without warning, Dang raised his weapon behind them as they cried, and—and I knew what he was planning to do. So, I couldn't bear it, and I looked away. Then I heard it. After that, I ran away from the Viet Cong that day, you know? I was too scared. He would have done the same to me." He hesitated and wiped sweat from his brow. "I fear Dang, but I hate him more. Maybe one day I kill him."

"Where did you go?" Eddie placed a hand on Vinh's shoulder again. "You made your way back to the village?"

"Not at first. I hid in the jungle for weeks. Nothing to live on, you know? Just buried myself among the thick trees and hoped . . ."

Vinh ran his fingers through his thick hair. "Then, I lived in a Montagnard village for a month, doing a few chores, lying low. After I thought it was safe, I slowly went back to my home. That's where I learned Mama-san had gone with you to the big base."

"And did you ever see Mama-san again?" Eddie asked.

Vinh wiped his forehead. "Yes, I also went to the big base in Chu Lai. I stayed there for a little while. I looked for you—of course, I did. But they said you had already left. And then Lieutenant Brighton got me a job." His eyes welled up again. "Mama-san died not long after I got there. I was sure she had waited for me to come back. And then she could go."

The lower corners of Eddie's mouth sagged as he dropped his head. "I loved that old woman too, Vinh."

He remembered when she took care of him after he escaped from Dang. It was Mama-san who got the word to Lieutenant Brighton that he was alive and at her hooch.

Tears streamed down his cheeks as he recalled how her eyes gleamed when she smiled and the way she said, *Eddie*. She was a good, kind woman.

He glanced at Vinh. "I really did love her. And hell, I'm sorry you had it so hard because of me."

"It wasn't your fault. It was the war. Nobody to blame."

Vinh said it in a resigned matter-of-fact way, almost the same way the farmers had spoken of repairing their huts and animal pens after the typhoon swept through his village. Eddie nodded slowly.

Eddie didn't agree at all. Someone was always to blame in such situations. But Vinh's way was the Vietnamese way, and he respected it.

"You're right, Vinh."

Now Vinh stood and faced Eddie.

"I'm what Americans refer to as boat people. I lived in Houston for several years before getting a sponsor in Austin." He hesitated as he gazed out the window. "I'm glad to be in America."

"I'm happy you are, too." Eddie embraced Vinh.

"What about your friend? I think you called him Mitch?" Vinh smiled. "I remember the night we all jumped into the animal pen and had buffalo dung all over us."

"Yes, I remember that night too. The next day Mama-san made us strip and washed our uniforms." Eddie chuckled. "But even Mama-san couldn't save my clothes. They still stank like I don't know what."

They laughed loudly.

"Do you still talk to your friend, Mitch?" Vinh asked.

"I wish I could say differently, but no. Sadly, he was killed a couple of months later near Quang Ngai."

Eddie wiped his eyes.

"You named your son after Mitch?" Vinh asked.

"Yes, I did. And Ronnie is named after another friend, Ronnie Porter. I don't believe you met him." Eddie glanced at the clock. "I guess it's time to get you home. You have school tomorrow."

•

As he sped along the road, he and Vinh continued to talk about Vietnam. Eddie turned his head sideways now and again, looking his friend in the eye as they conversed, barely believing he was sitting right there in the passenger seat. He could never have imagined this day.

He was distracted. He had his foot down on the gas and suddenly—*whoosh*—a silver dart-like object seemed to flash toward their windshield. Out of nowhere, a fast metallic car backed out of a driveway into the street. Eddie's foot rammed the brakes hard. The car slid and screeched, the smell of hot burning tires and the high-pitched tones of anguished cuss words permeating the air.

Their car somehow came to a halt as the other vehicle nonchalantly reversed out and sped away as if nothing at all had happened. Eddie almost wrenched his ankle from its socket with the force of the braking, and Vinh used both hands to push himself away from the passenger side console, afraid that stopping so fast would launch him through the windshield.

"Fuck!" Eddie spat, and then apologized, knowing the polite Vinh might be offended. "Sorry, sorry. Stupid, reckless driver. You okay, Vinh?"

"I am okay. But I think your seat is coming apart. You know, with the jolt." He pointed down, somewhere near Eddie's feet.

Caught in the shock of the near-miss, Eddie wasn't thinking straight.

So he kicked and scuffed around in the footwell to see what his friend had been referring to. Finally, his foot made contact with something hard, something metal.

"See, part of the car seat." Vinh nodded toward the floorboard.

Only, it wasn't, of course.

When Vinh stooped forward to take a better look at the very thing Eddie had forgotten he'd even stashed, Eddie's face reddened.

"Sorry, sorry," he said again. "Sorry, Vinh."

He didn't know quite what else to say.

He was sure Vinh did not like firearms much, and certainly would rather not know he was riding on top of one.

The carefully concealed pistol had flown out from under the seat, slid across the floor, and came to rest underneath the pedals. Eddie reached down and pulled it free.

"You have a gun?" Vinh asked, seemingly unaware he was stating the obvious. Vinh looked nervous, as if he momentarily wondered if Eddie was really the good man he believed he was.

Eddie's eyes flashed.

"Only for protection. Against Dang, you know? I keep it under my seat, as you saw. You know what he's like, Vinh . . ."

Eddie was chattering on, quite unsure where to stop.

Vinh wiped sweat from his brow. "Good to know."

Eddie looked uncertain. Was it good to know he had a gun? Or good to know it was for protection against a common enemy? He wished he knew.

But it would have to remain unspoken.

Vinh let the matter drop. It was none of his business.

He pointed at a home on the corner. "Take that driveway, Eddie."

Once Eddie steered the car into the driveway and stopped, he opened the door and stepped out. Ahead of them Eddie saw a small, well-kept wooden home of less than a thousand square feet.

"So, this is where you live?"

Vinh waited at the front of the car.

"Yes. I live here with three other families."

"Damn, Vinh, that doesn't sound good." Eddie hesitated. "How old are you now? You have to be older than seventeen."

He pulled out his wallet displaying his driver's license. "See, I'm almost nineteen. I graduate this year." Vinh smiled.

Eddie recalled that he'd been the same age when he'd gone off to war. He glanced at Vinh fleetingly, feeling a slight sadness that the teenager had experienced nothing but fighting ever since his birth. He couldn't imagine a lifetime of suffering that the horrors of war brought.

And if not suffering, then becoming hardened to it was even worse. A kid that young ought not to know the hardships of war. He should have been worried about his school grades, about slowly becoming a man, about drinking and women and having a fun time.

They walked along the sidewalk toward the house, the night air subdued between them as if they shared a secret that neither dared speak of. Flies and moths danced around a single streetlamp, oblivious.

There was some kind of smell, a stench in the air. The scent was of danger, and it made all the fine hairs on the back of Eddie's neck stand on end. It turned his guts and set him on edge. He recalled that smell from his time in Vietnam, and it brought back a hundred bad memories—but he also remembered that he was safe in Austin. He sighed heavily.

"You okay, Eddie?" Vinh asked.

"Yeah, I am, young Vinh. I am."

Eddie put his arm around Vinh's shoulders. "Look. I've been thinking while we were driving here. Why don't you come live with us? With me and Cheryl? Mitch and Ronnie can share a room for a while."

"I don't know." Vinh looked at the ground. "What about your wife?"

Eddie squeezed his shoulder. "Trust me. She wouldn't mind you staying with us. You saw her reaction when she met you." He lightly punched Vinh on the arm. "C'mon, say yes. You can move in this weekend. C'mon, Vinh . . ." He made it playful and punched Vinh again, making the boy laugh.

"Okay, okay. I'll move in with you. Thank you, Eddie."

CHAPTER 9

NOT THE CAR

Once Vinh moved into Mitch's room, the family settled into a routine that accommodated their new guest. Eddie knew that his two boys liked having Vinh around the house, and he was appreciative of how well Vinh treated his sons. He was a perfect fit.

Each morning after breakfast, Vinh rode with Eddie to take Mitch to school and then they went on to Austin High School. On the way home, they picked up both boys from the daycare facility. Eddie relished Vinh's companionship during the trips, their time to talk one-on-one.

One day a few weeks later, the Ford Fairmont turned into the parking lot right before the first bell was due to ring. "Damn, someone parked where I usually park." Eddie scanned the parking lot.

Vinh looked over his shoulder, checking out the car. "That's funny because it looks like your car that's parked there already."

But Eddie was distracted and paid the comment no attention.

"Found a spot. Let's hurry." Eddie parked across the lot, and then the teacher and student rushed to the classroom.

The students raised their eyes toward the door when the bell rang.

Eddie entered the classroom. Vinh followed behind and took his seat. The class applauded their teacher for making it to the room on time. They had observed his mad dash through the window.

"Thank you." Eddie smiled and bowed to the class. "I thank you."

The school day started like any other day. Eddie attempted to keep the students' attention for each of the one-hour classes. Some days he was successful, other days, not so much. He sought to improve the lessons whenever the students didn't stay involved.

When the last bell rang, the students hurried out of the classroom. Vinh stood by the doorway, waiting for Eddie to finish collecting his papers.

After several minutes Eddie looked toward the door. "Okay, let's go. I think I have everything."

"It's about time."

Vinh smiled, moving away from the entrance so Eddie could pass.

As Eddie and Vinh walked across the parking lot toward the car, an explosion rocked the peaceful high school campus. Out of sheer instinct, both hit the ground at the same time, lying prone, covering their heads.

Eddie peered back over his arm and saw the front of a car burning, black smoke billowing toward the sky as if released from a fiery furnace. Students were running in all directions, screaming, yelling. A few were silent as death itself, apparently in shock.

Car doors slammed and tires screeched as panicked drivers accelerated to leave the area. It was chaos in the parking lot, cars bumper to bumper, ramming this way and that, struggling to escape like cows in the slaughterhouse when they hear the first round fired. Eddie saw several students tumble to the ground while others jumped over them.

He leaped to his feet, rushing toward the burning car.

Behind him, on his heels almost, came Vinh.

The car was similar to his, the one that had parked in his regular spot. He spotted the driver, a young female student, stumbling out the open driver's door, her arms flailing, momentarily blinded. Eddie and Vinh each grabbed an arm, not needing to speak, knowing instinctively what was required. She whimpered, in too much pain or shock to speak or cry.

They walked her away from the burning car. She was happy to be led.

Eddie glanced over his shoulder, noticing the paint bubbling and peeling from the front of the Fairmont while the flames licked the hood of the vehicle. The glass had blown out and littered the pavement.

Once they were a safe distance from the fire, they lowered the girl to the pavement. She sobbed from the fear of almost being killed. Her body shook violently while Eddie quickly checked her for any visible wounds. "You're okay." Eddie smiled to reassure her. "I can't see any wounds."

"What happened?" she cried. "What happened?"

Eddie glanced around the parking lot.

"I don't know. But you're okay. It would've given you a jolt, so take it easy for a week or so. But otherwise—"

"Are you sure?" She wiped the black soot from her face.

He held her hand to reassure her. "Yes, I believe you are." He looked toward Vinh. "Don't worry, help will be here shortly."

Within minutes, teachers and students attempted to put the fire out with extinguishers. Eddie could hear the wails of fire department trucks and police sirens, seemingly not too far from the school.

"Looks like they got the fire contained." Vinh placed a hand on Eddie's shoulder.

Eddie scanned the parking lot. "Look at that red Cadillac pulling out into the main road." He pointed at the car. "I don't recall seeing that one before today." He shuddered.

The firetruck pulled into the parking lot near the smoldering car. Firefighters quickly began spraying the vehicle with retardant foam. Firemen worked around the car, looking for any hot spots.

Eddie signaled that he needed medical assistance for the girl, and two paramedics rolled a gurney with their equipment on top toward her. Eddie and Vinh stood back while they checked her over.

The older of the two glanced at Eddie and asked, "What happened?"

"She was in the driver seat when the car exploded. It could've been something with the fuel line, but I don't really know." Eddie took a deep breath. "Then Vinh and I helped her out of the car and brought her here. She's shaken, but alert." Eddie studied the paramedics as they worked on her. "I didn't find any external injuries, but, you know, we didn't remove any of her clothing. It's intact, at least."

Within minutes a tall, muscular police officer approached the group. "Are you a teacher?"

"Yes, I am," Eddie replied.

The officer glanced back at the smoldering car. "I heard you pulled the girl from the vehicle. Is that correct?"

"Yes, we helped her from the car. Then Vinh and I assisted her to a safe distance away. She appeared uninjured, but scared." Eddie wiped at the sweat dripping down his face. "The medics showed up a short time later."

The officer took down Eddie's contact details and nodded.

"Thanks, sir. If I need anything else, I'll be in touch."

Eddie glanced toward the girl. "Not a problem, officer. We'll head out then." Eddie decided it was time to leave. He didn't want anyone to know that he might be somehow associated with the exploding car.

On the drive home, Eddie and Vinh were quiet.

As the car pulled into the daycare parking lot, Vinh turned in his seat to eye Eddie. "You know that was meant for you, don't you?"

So, he had finally come right out and said what was passing silently between them both—something neither wished to talk about after leaving the school parking lot.

Eddie's eyes narrowed as he glanced at Vinh. "I know. Now someone else got injured because of me." He put the car in park. "Hell, that explosion could've killed a lot of people." When he opened the door, Eddie looked at Vinh before stepping out of the car. "Let's not tell Cheryl about this. She doesn't need the stress."

Vinh turned in his seat. "Okay, I won't say a word."

After the boys were seated, Eddie put the car into gear and steered onto the street. The boys must've sensed something was wrong. They typically laughed and talked on the trip home, but they were silent the whole way.

Once he pulled into the driveway, Cheryl burst out of the front door, racing toward the car. "I saw the news. It looked like your car, Eddie. D'you think it could've been someone trying to get to you, by—"

"Look, we're fine. So let's not talk about it tonight, okay?" Eddie caught Cheryl in his arms, swinging her around. "Anyway, it was a student's car." He lowered her to the ground. "All over with."

Cheryl stepped back, her eyes barely concealed her heightened anxiety. Her cheeks were flushed.

Clearly, the discussion was not over yet for Cheryl.

In fact, she had barely begun.

"The news said the explosion nearly killed that poor girl."

Eddie shot Vinh a glance and then shrugged his shoulders. "We suspect they wired the wrong car. They meant to kill us." He no longer felt that keeping this information from Cheryl was the right decision.

It was clear she already had it all worked out.

"Oh, my God, it was meant for you!" Cheryl cried. "I knew it!"

Once again, the fear had come looking for him. And fear had found him. His first instinct was to consider moving back to California to protect his family. But Eddie knew that it would be useless. Dang would surely find him.

He decided to keep that thought from Cheryl, too.

"You remember the man taking pictures of the car when we were in Little Saigon?"

Cheryl nodded that she did. "Yes, I do."

"I believe that's why they thought it was mine." Eddie stroked her hair.

After everyone was inside, the family fell into its nightly routine of eating dinner, bathing the boys, attempting to relax, and then heading to bed. This night, there was little conversation. Eddie noticed even the boys were quieter than usual.

•

The next morning, after a fitful sleep, Eddie sipped on his coffee while he surveyed the street through the kitchen window. It was like any other Saturday morning in the middle-class neighborhood. Within an hour, he knew he would hear the synchronized hum of lawnmowers. And once the last mower finished, the neighbors would start to wash their cars.

It was like some strange but well-orchestrated suburban dance, and everyone joined in, yet rarely did they speak to one another as they went about it.

He watched the mailman stop in front of the mailbox and leave the mail without getting out of the small white postal truck.

He then proceeded to the next box.

Eddie glanced at Cheryl while she read the paper. "The mailman came. I'll go get the mail."

"Okay, honey." She didn't look at him.

When he walked by Mitch, he ruffled his hair and then strolled out the door and down the drive. He pulled the lid down and removed the day's mail. A small manila envelope got his attention. He looked it over and noticed there wasn't a return address, but the postal mark was Austin.

Once he reached the porch, Eddie sat on a chair and pulled out his pocket knife. He carefully sliced the side of the envelope and turned it upside down to allow the contents to fall into his hand. It was a Polaroid photograph. His eyes focused on the picture, and he saw the burning car. His hands began to tremble. On the bottom edge, in a neat black script from a fountain pen read, "Missed this time. Next, we won't."

He slid the picture into the envelope and stuffed it into his jeans pocket. *I'm not showing this to Cheryl.* And this was one decision where he was sure he wouldn't change his mind.

After he entered the kitchen, he put the rest of the mail in front of Cheryl. "Nothing interesting today, as usual." Nothing about his face betrayed the deep-seated fear that gripped at his stomach and made him feel cold all over. He was used to masking things, so this was no different. But it felt worse now—because the fear was not for himself. He was afraid that Dang was out to get Cheryl and the boys.

Cheryl smiled. "Thanks, honey."

She trusted him, and he was lying to her again.

He hated it, hated having to do it.

Vinh entered the kitchen, stretching his arms toward the ceiling. He noticed Eddie's demeanor. "What's wrong?"

"We need to find Dang," Eddie muttered under his breath.

A TERRIFYING PHONE CALL

The last bell rang, followed by the shuffle and scrape of students packing books into bags, shoes scuffing along the floor, everyone keen to escape for the afternoon. "On your way out, make sure you leave your homework in the assignment box on my desk," Eddie announced, tapping some of the students on their shoulders as they filed past, dropping off their papers.

"No excuses, I expect to see homework from everyone. Every single person. Don't tell me the dog ate it, or that your best friend's sister's hamster died . . . Just leave the homework. And I hope it's good!"

Everyone liked Eddie and found him fair and amusing. The students sniggered at the joke about the hamster. If there was one thing that made kids laugh, it was always a hamster joke.

Sure, Eddie could be stern like a teacher should be, but he had compassion and was on the students' level. He was able to relate to everyone.

Students filed by him, dropping off their papers. He watched as the last of the kids walked out the door.

Vinh, as usual, stood at the doorway, always a little awkward about being the boy who went home alongside Eddie. Teacher's pet, some of the other students said.

Eddie packed his briefcase with the papers that he needed to grade before Monday. He looked forward to spending time with Cheryl and the boys. Weekends were family time in the Henderson home.

The crackle of the intercom system startled him. "Mr. Henderson, you have a phone call in the office," blared the speaker. "Mr. Henderson, a phone call in the office, please come now."

He smiled, thinking Cheryl must've called to have him pick up some groceries for the weekend. His smile got larger when he thought she might want him to grab a bottle of Jim Beam.

It'd been a while since he had a drink.

And it was the weekend, after all. He deserved one. Or two.

When Eddie strolled into the locker-lined hallway with its polished tile floor, he heard the sounds of laughter along with excited conversations, the jabbering of words spoken too fast, too animated, interspersed with the occasional shout of a student's name and a little push-and-shove.

Eddie acknowledged the kids in the hallway rushing to leave school. He only wished they had that sense of urgency in the classroom.

But they were so young, and he remembered those days. He couldn't hold it against them—after all, he was the same in his youth. It was when you got older, had kids and a wife, that was when you saw with fresh eyes.

While he brushed past a group of students standing in the office doorway he smiled and said, "Excuse me." His shoulders relaxed in obvious relief once he entered the quiet room without the throngs of students scurrying to leave. But now he had to dodge staff leaving for the day. Some of them were almost as eager and irrepressible as the kids.

He stopped at the secretary's desk. "I have a phone call."

"Yes, Mr. Henderson." She handed him the handset. "It's Professor Henderson. Your wife, I think?"

Eddie glanced around the office, then spoke.

"Hi, honey, what do you need me to pick up for you?" There was silence. "Cheryl?"

"Eddie . . ."

He heard a tremor in her speech. "Is there something wrong with one of the boys?" He lowered his voice. "Are you okay?"

"Eddie, I need you to come straight home. Don't pick up the boys. Don't bring them home. Please."

Her voice was almost a whisper.

His eyes narrowed. "What's wrong, Cheryl?"

"Just do as I say. Don't pick up the boys, and I mean all of them. I'll explain when you get here. Please."

His heart pummeled in his ribcage. His eyes shot to the clock.

"I'm on my way. Love you."

The phone call disconnected before he heard her say *I love you* back.

Panic gripped him as he placed the handset into the cradle. "Thank you," he said to the secretary, but his eyes were wide, and the only thing that flashed through his mind was that something was wrong. Something was very wrong. Eddie rushed out the door, running toward his car, his feet moving so fast he was afraid his shoes might fly off.

And now, unlike most school days, Vinh was waiting by the passenger door, a broad smile on his face. Eddie unlocked the door and took his seat in a rush. Vinh entered the other side and turned to Eddie again, waiting for the habitual "All set?" But it didn't come. Eddie's smile was missing too.

Eddie threw the car into gear, burning rubber as he flew out of the parking lot. He glanced at his passenger who was pinned back against his seat with the sudden acceleration. Eddie knew he didn't need to say anything to break the silence. Vinh had always been able to sense Eddie's panic, and though he might wonder what brought it on, he wouldn't say anything until Eddie did.

"Vinh, I'm dropping you off before we get home. Something is wrong with Cheryl. I don't want anyone there."

It sounded almost rude, dismissive of his friend. It was unusual.

Vinh clenched his jaw. "Take me with you. I can help."

"I can't. Cheryl said not to bring any of the boys home. That includes you. I don't know what it is, but something isn't right."

Eddie looked straight ahead but reached out sideways and touched Vinh's shoulder. "Please. Just understand."

Vinh nodded and remained silent. There wasn't really anything he could say, but his face, flushed and nervous, looked boyish now. Usually Eddie was a friend, almost an equal these days, but when he kept Vinh away from the problems, it only served to accentuate to Vinh that he was merely a kid. He wanted to help, but it was clear there was no place for a teen to assist in serious things—adult things.

He wanted to cry, but that wouldn't help anyone.

•

A million different thoughts ran through Eddie's mind, but he couldn't pinpoint what might be wrong. The boys were at daycare and Cheryl's pregnancy had proceeded without any problems, so what else was there?

Ray! Baby Ray! That must be it! Something's wrong with Ray. He accelerated, pulling onto Loop 1.

Less than a half-mile from his home, he pulled into a McDonald's parking lot. "Vinh, here's five dollars. Get something to eat. Stay here until I come back for you. Stay put, okay?"

Vinh took the bill. "Okay. But you sure you don't need me?"

"No, I'm not, but Cheryl said not to bring anyone." Eddie's eyes darted around the parking lot.

Vinh opened the door and stepped out.

"Come get me soon."

He looked lost, and five dollars was not much, not if he might be sitting there for hours on end.

"I will," promised Eddie, but his facial expression betrayed how his mind was already elsewhere. He sped away as soon as Vinh slammed the passenger door shut and, within seconds, the car was out of sight.

THE RUSH TO GET HOME

Once he turned onto the main road, Eddie was frustrated by the congested traffic that was moving too slowly. He zipped back and forth across the two lanes, overtaking on the left, passing on the right—he didn't much care.

Many drivers honked at him, and some made obscene hand gestures.

But Eddie noticed none of it. All he could see was the road and the many obstacles that seemed to have a will to stop him from getting home. Home, with Cheryl, where he needed to be. Right now.

When the upcoming light turned yellow, he accelerated right through the intersection, barely missing a pickup truck. There was no such thing as waiting for green lights in an emergency, even if he had no idea what could be amiss. After a right turn onto his street, he sped into the driveway, hitting the brakes so hard the car skidded and almost crashed into the garage door.

He slammed into park and opened the door in one motion. After his feet hit the ground, he ran toward the house.

"Cheryl, Cheryl!" Eddie hurtled into the living room, not noticing that the front door was already open. "Cheryl!"

Out of the corner of his eye, he saw a man thrust a stick out in front of him. Before he knew what happened, he tripped and flew through the air. Eddie landed hard, face-first, and slid several feet across the wood floor. He rolled onto his back and reached for his pistol.

Fuck, I forgot to grab it.

A boot pressed down on his chest.

Eddie looked up. His heart nearly stopped, right there, right then.

He found himself staring upward into a haggard, scarred face.

This was *the* face, the face of the man he loathed, the face he wanted to see bleed and squirm and writhe and die—it belonged to the one whose suffering and pain-filled demise he had long dreamed about. The marked face of this heinous man looming over him, impressed upon his mind for so long now, jolted him from his restless sleep and pursued him nightly in his tormented dreams. This face had been such a central part of his nightmares for so long it barely seemed possible to see it now, in the flesh.

The pupils of the man's eyes transported him way, way back, back to a time when he'd first seen them glow red with venom as the whites had seemed to grow smaller. This man—he was inhuman. The devil himself.

The man standing above him was older, ravaged by time. His skin creased, his gut pronounced.

But some features never changed.

Though the man had gray hair at his temples and was a little heavier, Eddie had no doubts. The slice Eddie had taken out of his cheek was a dead giveaway, but even if that hadn't been there, it could only be Dang.

"What the fuck are you doing in my home?" Eddie screamed. "Cheryl, where are you? Where are you?"

He squirmed and skidded on the polished floor, his back pinned while he fought in vain to rotate and get free. But he couldn't. He could only flail like an insect on its back, unable to right itself.

He reached up, clawing at the man's feet. He grabbed at the boot pressing on the center of his chest with both hands, twisting in one direction as hard as he could, his fingers digging into the seam where the upper of the soft leather boot met with the sole.

His short-cut fingernails dug, dug deeper, harder, struggling to get a hold, attempting to rip the foot away from his sternum. And more than that, he wanted to pull the man off his feet, slam him down on the hard floor and see him struggle. But for now, all he achieved was the pain and the horrific sensation, as if each fingernail was being ripped from its nail bed one by one. Still, he had a purpose. Eddie pulled and pulled on Dang's leg, harder still, pushing through his pain.

Dang tried to maintain his balance but wavered, wobbling on one leg.

"Fuck you, man," Dang cried. "Fuck you!"

His other foot was sliding now, unable to stay put.

Eddie detected Dang's weakness and pulled and tugged with every ounce of strength. And finally, he saw results.

Dang couldn't counter the force Eddie relentlessly applied. At first, he tried kicking out. But with one foot caught fast now, he failed. He realized he'd made a grievous mistake as he slid and fell hard, hitting his head on the end table and breaking it as he crashed to the floor. The ceramic fruit bowl that had been sitting on the table exploded, sending shards everywhere. Some dug themselves deep into Dang's exposed neck and pierced his back through his shirt. His face grimaced in pain. For now, he appeared incapacitated.

Eddie grabbed the end of the sofa, pulling himself to a standing position. For a moment, he stood and caught his breath, staring down at Dang as if the creature on the floor was no longer a threat. Dang seemed preoccupied, holding his head one second, then flicking at his injured skin attempting to get the shards out of his flesh. He was too engrossed in his pain to even look up at Eddie.

"Cheryl, where are you?" Eddie called.

"I'm over here. Eddie, help me!" Cheryl cried from the hallway. And she was not alone.

There was a second man, his presence explaining why Dang did not even try to break through his pain to make a vicious comeback. It seemed he knew his accomplice would do whatever it took to keep Eddie down and achieve their goal.

The second man was also Vietnamese, but more heavyset than Dang. He pushed Cheryl into the living room, restraining her red-raw wrists behind her back with his hands.

Tears streamed down her cheeks leaving a trail of black mascara. Her eyes were wide with fear, terrified, a look Eddie had never seen on her face.

Eddie started to move toward Cheryl. He heard a loud *thwack* and then pain exploded in his brain. His legs buckled and he fell to his knees. A third man then stepped between Eddie and Cheryl.

Struggling to focus, he waited for the pain to stop.

Then he recognized the man. It was the Viet Cong teenager who'd carried the bamboo stick when he was a prisoner, and beat Ray and him with it repeatedly.

Eddie wasn't surprised to see Canh was with Dang—they were equally cruel. And now the man was no longer a teenager, but a short, muscular adult with a sneer plastered on his acne-scarred face.

After Dang struggled to his feet, he took slow steps toward Eddie and Canh.

He bent down and looked at Eddie.

"I told you I would punish you." He grabbed Eddie's hair, lifting his head to look into his eyes. "Why were you looking for me?" Dang tightened the grip on Eddie's hair. "Why couldn't you leave things alone?"

Eddie attempted a laugh. "Fuck you, motherfucker!"

Dang smiled and released his hold on Eddie's hair, letting his head slump forward. He stood again and moved toward Cheryl. "I remember telling you that your wife was beautiful." He traced his finger down her left cheek. "She is even more beautiful in person."

"Don't touch me!" Cheryl screamed. "Eddie, help me!"

"Leave her alone." He attempted to leap to his feet, but the man with the stick struck him across the left shoulder. Eddie fell back to his knees. His mind screamed as the pain shot through his shoulder, arm, and back. He heard the intruders cursing and shouting at him in Vietnamese.

Tears rolled down his cheeks as he looked at Cheryl.

"You better not hurt her, Dang. Fuck you." Eddie muttered. "Stay tough, Cheryl. We'll be okay. We'll be okay," he repeated, as if trying to convince himself more than her. "We'll get out of this, honey, believe me."

Despite his words, a sense of helplessness crept through Eddie's mind.

He watched the man holding Cheryl and then saw Dang edge forward, touching her, making a show of running his fat, grubby hands down Cheryl's cheek, enjoying every second. Hatred washed through every sinew of Eddie's body. Dang slowly moved his hands around her body, watching Eddie for the desired reaction. "Nice wife you have, Eddie. Mmm, she feels good. Real good . . ."

Eddie scanned the room but couldn't find a way out without Cheryl getting harmed. And worse, he realized there wasn't a way out—period. Any move he took would seriously endanger the one person he loved more than anything in the world. For now, anyway, Dang was firmly in control. He might as well be locked in the bamboo cage.

Dang placed his hand on Cheryl's stomach.

"I see your wife is with child. It is a shame. Such a shame . . ."

Eddie's distraught mind ran away with itself. Inside, he whimpered and wept and cursed, wishing he could beat his fists into Dang's face, but externally, he had to appear calm. Any slight crack in his composure and Dang would have him where he wanted him.

Cheryl, though, did all the whimpering and weeping openly for him. Her body visibly shook as great tears ran down her cheeks.

"Don't you dare touch my baby!" Cheryl tried to pull away, but Dang held her by her long hair as he stared at Eddie.

"Well, doesn't look like your good wife here wants to play with me." His lips formed a pout. "Maybe she will later, when it's me and her. But meanwhile, I think it's time for a little reminiscing, Eddie. How about we remember the good old days? What do you think about that?" Again, his cold gaze pierced Eddie's face, looking for weakness, testing him. "Remember the young boy, the one who fed you and gave you water?"

How could Eddie ever forget?

The memory of the young boy flashed through Eddie's mind, as if replaying a movie, the long chain of flickering images coming and then fading away. He recalled the youngster being quiet but friendly and compassionate to him and Ray when they were prisoners. Somewhat polite, if he remembered correctly—but in a good way. A way that Westerners rarely were these days

This was the same Viet Cong child that had given them food and water. He'd even tied Ray's boots for him.

"Yes, I do remember him," Eddie muttered. If he refused to speak, then that would seem disloyal to the boy. He deserved recognition.

"Well, he was my son." Dang released Cheryl's hair. "I had to kill him when he let you escape. So, you have yourself to thank for his death. Only yourself to blame. How does that feel now, Eddie? You must've known what I'd do to him when I found out. Reckon that makes you as much of a killer as I am. Shame, though, because he liked you." He ran his finger along the scar on the right side of his face. "Remembering old times together is fun, though, isn't it, Eddie?"

Cheryl sobbed even harder, her eyes as wide as they could get. She stared at Eddie, pupils boring into his, as if to say, *Did you really let a boy die so you could go free?*

Eddie gazed at Dang with disbelief and horror. His stomach churned and his mouth watered as if he was about to vomit. If it was true that Dang murdered the boy, he hoped and prayed that it'd been quick and merciful, at least. But he knew it wouldn't have been.

Dang was only interested in pain and suffering.

"You didn't have to do that. He was a good kid, not like you."

He wasn't about to tell him that it was Vinh that had let him escape that day, not the boy who turned out to be his son.

"Yes, I did. And you made me do it. You cost me my son." He signaled to the man with the bamboo stick. "So now, in exchange, I'm going to take away your child. Then we'll be even, Eddie, right?"

Dang stepped away from Cheryl, clearing space around her. The man holding onto her merely tightened his grasp, keeping her arms pinned behind her back so she couldn't move.

She fought and squirmed to break his hold, but he was too strong.

"*Cánh*," Dang called out.

The third man, the one with the stick, stepped in front of Cheryl, flexing and bending the thick cane between two hands as if demonstrating.

"Eddie!" Cheryl cried. "Oh, my God, don't do this. Please, not my baby. Oh God, please, please . . ."

With wide eyes, Eddie surveyed the room, struggling to figure out how to stop what was about to happen. The pain of losing Cheryl or Ray, or both of them, washed over him.

"No, Dang, don't, I'm begging you. I'll give you anything you want."

"This is what I want." Dang waved his hand back at Cheryl. "I want to see your kid taken away like you took mine."

Dang gave a command. "*Giết em bé.*"

He smiled. "Kill the baby."

With a blur, Eddie saw the bamboo stick slice through the air, heard the whoosh of air and the sharp *thwack* as it hit Cheryl in the stomach with full force. She screamed. The man holding her released his grasp, and she fell to the floor, holding her stomach and crying in pain.

"My baby, my baby!" She curled into a fetal position. "Eddie, help Ray. Please help Ray, Eddie!"

Eddie began to cry. The feeling of helplessness overcame him as he watched Cheryl beg for mercy, for the life of their unborn son.

•

Eddie struggled against the fourth man who held him tight in a rough bear hug from behind, ensuring he couldn't move a limb. In fact, Eddie could hardly breathe. Eddie's face showed a mass of emotions: rage at his helplessness, burning hatred, nausea, and shame that he couldn't protect his wife.

He wanted to call out to her, to say something that would make her feel better, more reassured. But even that was pointless and senseless. How could he reassure her in a scenario where she might get killed, or where—at best—her body would be beaten black and blue to the point that her son's lifeless form would slide unmoving from her belly, aborted?

How could reassurance even be possible for him to give? Words were meaningless; they would only heighten how powerless he was to act. A shadow of a real man.

A man should be able to protect his family.

A shot rang out in the room as a bullet slammed into the wall, then ricocheted, scarcely missing Dang's head. The room became eerily quiet as the men's eyes flashed around the place for a glimpse of the shooter. Then they all ducked at once and scrambled for cover like young chickens surprised by a predator.

The man that held Cheryl dived for the floor, pulling Cheryl against him—not to protect her, but to avoid letting her loose. She lay pressed between the hardwood floor and her attacker. His giant hands grasped her wrist tightly, so much so that her skin was about to peel away. As he jumped to his feet, his free hand reached down into his waistband to pull out a pistol. He aimed it at the shooter.

Another shot came from somewhere out of sight and Dang's man with the pistol spun around, wincing in pain and grabbing at his left shoulder, holding onto it for dear life. The gun dropped to the floor and Cheryl winced. But it did not go off. Whoever was shooting in Eddie's favor had managed to hit his target. Although Eddie thought it would have been better to see the guy's brains splatter the wall.

Way, way better.

But blood seeped from beneath the man's fingers and dripped to the floor, slowly at first, but then becoming a torrent of bright redness that splashed on the floor and into Cheryl's hair.

The sound of sirens filled the afternoon air.

Dang barked orders in Vietnamese and the men fled out the back.

Cheryl was free at last.

Eddie turned and saw Vinh standing in the doorway holding the pistol Eddie kept under the seat of his car.

Eddie crawled toward his injured wife. "Cheryl, hang on. Help is on the way." He looked toward Vinh. "Come here. Now!"

Vinh rushed to Eddie's side.

"Give me the gun. I fired the shots, do you understand? You got here after they ran away. Do you understand? Say it!" Eddie looked into Vinh's eyes. "Say it back to me."

Vinh reached for Cheryl's hand. "I heard two shots when I approached the house and found you like this. I didn't see anyone."

"Good. Stick with that story no matter what." Eddie placed his hand on Vinh's shoulder. "Thank you. You saved us all. You saved my kid . . ."

Vinh nodded silently, as if overcome by emotion and uncertainty.

Eddie's focus switched to Cheryl.

"Cheryl, it'll be okay, the police are coming. We'll get you to the hospital. Hang on." Eddie wept as he pulled her into his arms. "I'm sorry, Cheryl, I'm so sorry."

Cheryl moaned as she slid closer against Eddie. Her body trembled in agony. "Help Ray!" Her voice sounded agonized, plaintive, and then ended in a short gasp.

When she looked up at Eddie her eyes rolled back.

Blood started to pool on the floor between her legs.

THE INTERROGATION BEGINS

Four police officers burst through the open doorway, yelling, "Police, police!"

One headed for Vinh with hate in his eyes while the other three checked each room. Eddie assumed the first was a Vietnam veteran who only saw a gook sitting next to Eddie.

Eddie deftly positioned Vinh behind him as he held onto Cheryl. "He's my son—he's my son," Eddie yelled while pulling Vinh in closer. "He's not the shooter. He's good . . ."

The officer stopped in his tracks, staring at Eddie. "Is the house clear?"

"House is clear," Eddie replied.

"You sure?"

The sound of heavy footsteps on the wooden floors confirmed the other officers were scanning every room.

"They left," Eddie glanced down the hallway. "I got one guy."

"What happened?" the police officer asked as he holstered his weapon.

"There were four intruders, held me and my wife and then beat the fuck out of her. I shot twice, wounding one of them. That's my gun lying there." Eddie pointed at the pistol. "They really hurt my wife. She's pregnant and she's bleeding badly. We need a doctor now."

The officer put his hand on Eddie's shoulder.

"The ambulance is pulling into the driveway, sir."

The paramedics rushed into the house and, at a nod from the officer in the room, started tending to Cheryl. "Can you stand?" one asked her gently as a female paramedic listened to the baby's heartbeat.

"I don't . . . I don't think so," Cheryl cried. "Save my baby, please."

They brought in a gurney from outside and three paramedics lifted Cheryl onto it as she writhed in pain.

"Can't give you any painkillers, ma'am, because of the risk to the—"

"Oh, sweet Jesus!" she cried. "Stop talking and get me to the hospital!"

They wheeled Cheryl out as fast as they'd entered.

She was sobbing, crying out for Ray, cursing now and then.

Nobody paid attention to her graphic expletives, but they couldn't ignore her blood-soaked clothing or the thick smell of iron filling the space around her. Her pain was more than physical—it was a deep mental anguish that ripped through her body and soul.

Eddie cried at the sight and sound of her, but wiped away his tears so the police wouldn't see his vulnerability. He was alone and helpless, and the room suddenly seemed hopelessly empty, almost as if Cheryl and the baby maybe wouldn't be coming back. She was in the ambulance now, being tended to before they set off.

The shock of the last hour or so was setting in and Eddie could hardly move. He didn't know what to do with himself. He should have tried to get in the ambulance with his wife. But he didn't— couldn't—get his head together even to realize that.

It was not just the trauma of today that was so debilitating. Every trauma he had ever suffered now pushing itself to the forefront. Every shooting, every painful death he had witnessed, every scream from a dying soldier.

"Should I—you know? Should I go join my wife?" he asked finally, somewhat flustered and dripping in sweat. His face was pale and blotchy with emotion. The officer stared at him as though he couldn't believe what he was hearing.

"Sir, there's been a shooting right here in this house. I think you need to stay where you are. You get me?"

"Yeah. I get you."

He took a deep breath, exhausted, confused, humiliated at what Dang had put them through. Mostly, he was ashamed of being unable to protect his wife as she deserved.

"Go to the kitchen, make a strong coffee, sit yourself down, and a detective will be with you shortly," the officer said.

When Eddie moved toward the kitchen, the officer's voice came again. "Oh, sir?"

"Yes?" Eddie turned to look back.

"None of this—this scuffle, or whatever you call it, happened out there in the kitchen, right? 'Cause, you know, we need to be sure that when the crime scene officer gets here the areas have been kept clear for forensics."

"Right."

Nothing more was said. The officer simply nodded, letting Eddie go.

Eddie went into the kitchen and flicked on the coffee pot—but his mind was elsewhere. After the boiling water filled the pot, Eddie noticed he forgot to add the coffee grounds. His mind was one hell of a mess. Coffee was a no-go, as he simply wasn't capable of making it. He pulled out a chair from the kitchen table and sat patiently as requested.

He picked at his hands, inspected his fingers front and back, turned back his shirt cuffs. Then he sighed deeply and rested his head in both cupped hands. His foot tapped impatiently.

Cheryl, Cheryl, Cheryl . . . and baby Ray. Please, God, please let them be okay. Please let them be fine. His foot started to tap faster and faster, sending a tsunami of shudders through the poorly made wooden chair.

After several minutes, Vinh entered and sat down next to Eddie. The chair legs made a scraping sound against the tiled floor. Eddie cringed, startled by every tiny noise.

They avoided looking at each other, each afraid that one of them might give the detective a clue as to who had fired the pistol.

Eddie had also decided not to tell the police who the intruders were. What would happen to Dang? He might get off or go to jail for a short period, and then he'd come looking—or his cronies would come looking—even more vicious-minded than before.

Even worse, Dang could turn things around, say he had been invited and that Eddie had suddenly pulled a gun on him because he'd mistaken him for someone else. And that things got out of hand. He would find a way to make himself the victim.

So, that wouldn't achieve a thing. Lies came quickly and cheap to Dang, and if ever there was a man who could lie until he even believed the goddamn stories himself, it was surely Dang.

Anyway, Eddie still wanted to exact his revenge and keep his promise to Ray Laurel. The only way he could do that was to lie to the police now.

A bald, older man wearing a wrinkled brown suit took a seat at the table. "Good evening, Mister Henderson. I'm Detective Anderson."

Eddie extended a hand.

"If you don't mind, I won't shake." The detective didn't move. "Forensics . . . We'll need to examine your skin in some detail."

"Oh. Sure," Eddie answered, withdrawing his hand and shaking his head. This sure was confusing.

"Need to ask some questions, can I get right into it?" Anderson asked.

"Sure, go ahead." Eddie gazed off into the living room.

The detective placed a notepad and pen on the table. "Start from the beginning. Tell me in your own words what happened. Everything you remember."

Any other time, that phrase *tell me in your own words* would have made Eddie laugh. It was a joke he'd once shared with Ray Laurel.

But who else's words could a man use except his own? Now, not even a tiny smirk would come to his face. It was hard to hold back the emotion.

"All I know is when I got home from school there were four men in the house." Eddie shifted in his seat. "They hurt my wife."

The detective made a note on his pad.

"That's a bit too brief. Can you go into detail please? They hurt your wife? What do you mean by that?"

"I don't honestly know. It happened so fast, a blur, you know? But she was down on the floor, and she was screaming and crying and saying over and over that they were hurting her. One guy had her head by the hair, and she looked pretty beaten up already."

"So, is that when you shot at them?"

"Yeah. No. Well, I fired two shots." Eddie sat back in his seat. "It was later . . . They took a stick and beat her with it, on the stomach where the baby was. It was too much, you know? Too much."

"It must've been." The detective made a note in his pad. "That's a lot to take in. So, you fired twice in succession?"

"Yeah, missed the first shot, my hand was shaking that much, so it went way wide. But I wounded one in the shoulder with the second shot." He glanced at Anderson. "He was pulling a gun on me too though, had his hand on his waistband and I'd seen it tucked in there. Plus, he still had Cheryl, and he might have shot her instead of me."

"So, you always carry a weapon?" the detective asked.

Eddie's jaw went tight.

"No, I bought it over a month ago and I'd left it in the car. Careless, I know. Guess I knew my wife wouldn't approve. Anyway, I was bringing it into the house to put it away." Eddie stared the detective in the eye, knowing it made for a greater show of honesty. "That's why I had it with me. I guess I was lucky."

Anderson smiled. "Yes, you were. Seems you were fortunate. It could've been a whole lot worse. We see home invasions that go terribly wrong." The officer was about to say more but shut up.

Eddie was shaking all over again.

The officer placed the pen down on the pad. "Okay, well, let's not focus on would haves and could haves. Fact is, you're okay. You're alive, you're not badly injured, and we have to hope your wife will be fine too. I'll find out for you soon. But first, what about your friend here?"

Eddie shot Vinh a side glance.

"I dropped Vinh off at McDonald's on the way home. You know how teenagers are always hungry. It's only a couple of blocks from the house." Eddie's eyes narrowed. "Vinh showed up right after the intruders left."

"Can you describe the men?" the detective asked.

Eddie sat up in his chair. "All four were Asian. That's all I know."

The detective shifted his gaze at Vinh.

"Is that correct, they were Asian?"

"I didn't see anyone. I don't know what the intruders looked like." Vinh stared into the detective's eyes and looked as if he was about to cry.

Good ploy, Eddie thought, though he was unsure if the emotion was real.

If I cry, he won't give a shit. But when a boy cries, it's gonna remind him of his kids. Let's hope he has some, anyway.

"I was really scared," Vinh cried. "And all I could think was, I went for a McDonald's while this was happening to them. And, like, it's my fault I wasn't there, my fault no one protected them."

"Your fault no one protected them?" the detective asked. "You're young. How could you protect them? You carry a firearm too?"

Eddie cringed. Vinh cringed.

Eddie's sidelong glance emerged again, but he hoped the cop wouldn't pick up on it. Damn, Vinh needed to answer what he asked, not keep on and on, embellishing things and digging himself into a deeper, darker hole.

And still, the questioning went on until finally, crime scene officers showed up after about an hour. Eddie felt wrung dry, like a dishcloth that was over-used, boil-washed, wrung out, dried, re-used, boiled again. There was no substance left in him. He couldn't see the woods for the trees.

He wanted to put his head down on the tabletop and sleep, and hope that he would wake to find himself and Cheryl hunkered down on the bedroom floor again, and that it had all been a nightmare.

But it wasn't. And Cheryl was in the hospital and God only knew what sort of a state he would find her in once the police finally let him go.

For an hour, there were detectives, crime scene personnel, and police officers walking throughout the house, taking notes and pictures. When the investigators finished, they packed up and left.

It seemed like hours to Eddie before the house was empty.

LIFE AND DEATH

Eddie sat at the kitchen table in silence, staring into the living room where a dark pool of blood soaked into the floor. The intruder's blood? Cheryl's?

He didn't care to think.

In a daze, Eddie turned to Vinh. "Let's get to the hospital."

When he turned to leave the kitchen, his shoulders slumped as his eyes searched the destroyed living room once again.

Eddie stepped around the broken end table as he looked back with a mournful gaze at the pool of blood. He resembled a soldier that had been in a horrific firefight with the enemy. This night would haunt him forever.

On the way out the front door, Eddie saw many of his neighbors gather along the sidewalk in front of the house. He spotted Missus Dalton.

"Missus D., I don't suppose you could pick up Mitch and Ronnie from the daycare and watch them until I get home?"

He nervously avoided the stares from his neighbors.

"Yes, you and Vinh go on ahead. I'll get the boys and take care of them. You take care of Cheryl." She patted him on the shoulder. "If you need me to take care of the kids overnight, you let me know, okay?"

He choked and the tears he had been holding back finally started to escape his eyes and roll down his face. "Okay. Thanks."

That was the thing about men and crying. Eddie had noticed it before. They could keep anything inside, no matter what, until someone showed a little bit more compassion than they were expecting, that sliver more of humanity. That was always the catalyst for a man to break down.

The small gesture from his kindly neighbor broke his resolve.

As Eddie backed the car out of the driveway, the crowd parted to let the car pass. He and Vinh drove to the hospital in silence.

Eddie kept replaying the events in his head, seeking to see how he could've changed the outcome.

Tears welled again in his eyes. He felt less than a man—less, even, than a boy. There was so much that was deeply emasculating about being unable to do a thing to stop your wife from getting beaten.

•

Once at the hospital, Eddie and Vinh waited for Cheryl to come out of surgery. Eddie wondered why it was taking so long.

"When they had us separated, did you tell the police what I told you to say?" Eddie asked.

Vinh looked at the floor. "Yes, I did. I'm sure they believed me."

"Good. If they question us anymore, stick with the same story. Don't change a word." Eddie put his arm around Vinh's shoulders. "Thank you again for saving my life a second time—and for saving Cheryl."

"Dang is evil. He'll be back." Vinh shifted in his seat. "I'm sorry Cheryl got hurt. She's a good person and doesn't deserve to know the pain of war."

"Let's get something straight here." Eddie pulled Vinh in closer. "What happened to Cheryl was not the pain of war. That was senseless violence, pure and simple. War . . . war has a purpose, even when there's pain. What we went through, that was no pain of war thing. Not by a long shot. And I hope you get where I'm coming from. Dang is a fucking cruel, bloodthirsty pig. Don't forget that. War has nothing to do with it."

"Sorry," Vinh whispered. "I know. It was only words. I wanted to make you feel better. I'm sorry."

Eddie's gaze fell to the floor. "Look, I gotta ask you something, and no bullshit now. Tell me the truth."

"Okay."

"Did Dang kill his son after I escaped?"

"Yes, he did. He was one of the two soldiers I told you about at your house after that first dinner." Vinh's shoulders slumped at the memory. "It was an execution."

"Fuck. I'm sorry you had to experience all that at such a young age. Hell, at any age." Eddie stood and put a hand on Vinh's shoulder.

The door from the surgical area opened, and a doctor still wearing surgical scrubs approached the two men.

Eddie's heart went to his throat. He couldn't breathe, and his pulse raced so fast that it seemed his veins would burst.

"Mister Henderson?" the doctor asked.

Eddie moved toward the doctor. "Yes, I am."

The doctor stopped in front of Eddie. "Your wife is out of surgery, and she is doing fine."

A sense of relief flooded his body. He no longer needed to hide behind a mask of bravado. Tears welled in his eyes.

"Thank God. How's Ray? I mean, the baby?"

The doctor glanced down the hallway then back at Eddie. "Mister Henderson, you know, at times like this, we need to find peace where we can. Small mercies, you know?"

Eddie didn't understand. "So, you're saying the baby's fine too?"

"I'm sorry. The baby didn't make it. But let's all be thankful the good Lord saw fit to bring your wife safely through it."

Once the doctor's words sank in, Eddie's world collapsed. The pain came and went in waves. "I need to see Cheryl."

The doctor stared deep into Eddie's eyes.

"You need to know that your wife may experience many emotions, such as disbelief, anger, guilt, and depression. She may look for someone to blame, and she may lash out. The sense of bonding between a mother and her baby can be strong, and that can get in the way of reason sometimes. So, take whatever she says as a sign of her distress and her loss. Nothing more. I'm saying this as a woman and a mom, as well as a doctor."

Eddie wiped at a tear. "I understand. But I want to see her."

"Of course, follow me." The doctor turned and walked along the hallway until she reached an open door. "This is her room. Please only stay for a couple of minutes. She needs rest."

Eddie nodded. He squeezed through the doorway.

"Cheryl," he whispered.

Cheryl looked toward her husband and raised her hand. "I'm sorry. Ray . . . our little Ray of sunshine. He didn't make it."

"You have nothing to be sorry for—it's my fault." Eddie's gaze went to the doorway. "I brought the fight to our door . . . to you."

He took her hand into his and sobbed.

"Yes, you did." She moved her hand from his grasp and placed it on her belly, where Ray had thrived and kicked and been healthy.

"Cheryl, I didn't know this would happen."

She stared at him. "How are Mitch and Ronnie? Where are they?"

"They're fine. Missus Dalton has them. Don't worry." He sat on the edge of the bed. "Vinh is in the waiting area."

Cheryl wiped the tears that dripped off Eddie's cheeks. "It was Vinh who saved us, wasn't it?"

Eddie hesitated. "Yes, he did." He didn't want to talk about what happened, not now. "I had Vinh tell the police that he got there after the intruders left." He gazed into her eyes. "I didn't tell the police anything about what really happened. What good would it do? Even if Dang went to jail, he would be out in a couple of years. We'd still have the same problem. And anyway, he'd likely make up a story. He's a—well, there are no words to say what he is."

She nodded slowly, silently.

Without speaking a word, she pulled the blanket up to her shoulders.

He stroked her cheek. "I'm so sorry about Ray."

They were stupid words. He was sorry about the baby that he had a part in killing? Sorry about it? It was all too much for Cheryl.

She stared out the window at a world that had no meaning now, not right in this second. The world was gray and empty, like her belly.

"Eddie . . ." She wept, breaking down. "I don't know what I'm going to do without my Ray. He didn't deserve this." Cheryl wiped at tears. "I lost my baby."

"Our baby," Eddie whispered.

"My baby," she murmured back. "I told you not to mess with Dang."

The doctor was right.

Cheryl held Eddie responsible for what happened and he could never live with that.

Eddie had no words that would console her. "I'm here for you." He sat on the bed next to her, taking her hand. "I love you."

He kissed her cheek.

Cheryl squirmed to raise her body and motioned for Eddie to bend lower. "Eddie, shut the fuck up. Go kill the motherfucker that killed our Ray." She whispered in his ear. "Kill Dang!"

EVERYONE IS HOME

Once Eddie and Vinh returned home from the hospital, they began to repair the house, intent on erasing every cruel stain left behind. In the evenings, they worked together on patching the bullet hole in the wall and then painted their handiwork. The blood from Cheryl and the man Vinh had shot soon disappeared.

Now, it looked as if nothing terrible had ever happened there; it was fresher and cleaner than before. Cheryl would be able to settle back in, or so Eddie hoped. He was anxious, guilt-ridden, and fearful.

This place had to be perfect when she arrived home.

After a day of searching, Eddie found an end table to replace the broken one. He hoped to have the house looking like it had before Dang intruded into their lives.

While he sat in his recliner, Eddie rested his head in his hands.

Cheryl's screams and tormented cries echoed in the room.

He picked up the television remote, curling his fingers tightly as if squeezing Dang to death. His knuckles began to turn white as he gritted his teeth, his face flushing deep red. He rubbed at his sweaty brow and unkempt hair as he stared into space. He felt dead inside, swimming in a sea of hatred, pent-up aggression, and unspent tears.

There was absolutely no doubt his actions had only compounded the mess. Now, not only did he hate Dang as usual, but to add to his regret, hindsight, and self-loathing, he also hated himself for not saving baby Ray. It was his failure as a father, as a man.

He could almost reconcile things, knowing that he had done his best under the given circumstances. But in the back of his mind—or frequently in the forefront—there would always be the awareness that without his stupid interventions, Dang would never have shown up at the house to begin with.

Eddie decided to recognize it as his failure, but he would try not to carry a burden of guilt with him for the rest of his days.

It was too late for remorse and self-pity.

It was over, put to bed.

Unless, of course, Dang showed up again, as no doubt he would.

He needed to free himself from the guilt and kill Dang before more damage could be done, physically or psychologically, to him and Cheryl.

Vinh touched his shoulder. "We'll get them, Eddie. You and me."

"Yes, we will." Eddie looked up with hate radiating from his eyes. "I'm going to kill Dang and Canh."

After he said those words, Eddie realized that it was this same intent to kill Dang that had caused this mess. So now he was right back at the beginning—only with a massive loss on his hands and in his heart—the death of baby Ray.

"And I'm going to help you," Vinh promised again.

•

Eddie changed his schedule so he could get Ronnie to daycare first and then drop Mitch off at school before he and Vinh drove to Austin High. Although it was harder without Cheryl at home, they managed to get by.

The days blurred; Cheryl was still recovering in the hospital. The beating to her stomach had been so severe that when the doctor performed the surgery, there had been massive internal bleeding. She needed to heal, and getting out of bed would put her torn stomach muscles under far too much strain. Eddie would have to get by without her for at least another week.

While having McDonald's happy meals for dinner one evening, Vinh talked with and teased the boys. Eddie knew they missed their mother.

He watched the three boys eating and laughing. Vinh's position in the family was becoming more and more evident. He was like a son.

"Vinh, thank you for all you've done."

He stopped laughing. "I didn't do anything that you wouldn't do." The corners of Vinh's lips tugged into a strained smile. "I remember how you cared for my mother and Mama-san, and how you helped the people of my village."

Eddie retained a vivid memory of the day he'd found Mai, Vinh's mother. It was several days after the typhoon had come, and the First Platoon was moving its way through the village, slowly parting the strewn debris to create paths. Eddie found the woman lying in a pool of blood with Vinh standing over her, crying.

The VC had killed her. The platoon went off then, deciding to leave the village to search for the enemy that had slain her and the others.

None of them deserved to die, to be so humiliated and slaughtered there, in front of their babies and their children.

"I remember your mother well. Mai was a beautiful and caring woman. She loved you very much." Eddie's eyes glistened. "Anyway, whatever I did for you and Mama-san, you have returned tenfold. Thank you, Vinh. You're a good man and a loyal friend."

The sound of the phone ringing pierced through the kitchen.

Everyone stopped talking. Nowadays, even the little boys were on edge, their nerves alerted to something terrible that must've happened here in the house, in their safe space. Mom was gone, and Dad was in pieces most of the time. All they could do was hug their father and say, "Don't cry."

Eddie walked around the table and lifted the handset.

"Hello, Henderson residence."

"Hi, honey. It's been a long time coming, but you can come and get me in the morning," Cheryl paused. "I want to see my boys."

Eddie's smile beamed from one side of his face to the other.

"We can't wait to see you. The boys want to talk to you. Love you."

Eddie let Mitch and Ronnie talk to their mom.

While the boys chatted on the telephone to their mother, Eddie felt more optimistic than he had in a long time. Dang and his men had taken a lot from him, but with Cheryl coming home, the family would be stronger. At last, there was a light in his heart that had been absent yesterday. Maybe it was the spark he needed to reignite the optimism and anticipation. He smiled—this feeling hadn't surfaced in days.

He hadn't been sure it could ever return.

●

The next morning, Eddie picked Cheryl up at the hospital. She nestled herself gingerly on the back seat of the car, stretching full length with a soft blanket tugged across her. She smiled a little but seemed lost, defeated. The drive home was quiet, and regret washed over Eddie every time he glanced at Cheryl, imagining what was inside her head.

He longed to go back and do things differently. But of course he couldn't, and he had inadvertently managed to destroy something sacred and precious, something that would never return to them.

The only solace he could take was in the fact that she seemed to forgive him—at least, superficially so. He knew it would take time.

And then there was the knowledge—the hope—that baby Ray was being looked after someplace by Ray Laurel. *Gawddamn it!*

He chuckled.

He was not a religious man at all. Heaven was a place people made up to make themselves feel better in times of need. But even in his own time of need, he had been unable to believe it was there.

So, baby Ray's energy was floating someplace now, tuning into endless *gawddamn its* from his namesake.

That was as far as he could make himself think or believe.

Once Cheryl was established back at home, the family attempted to get back into their routine. But Eddie knew his wife didn't—couldn't—forget what had happened and simply move forward. It would never be like before.

He sensed her sadness over losing Ray and the hate she held for Dang. But he did his best to get Cheryl to move past that terrible night.

After dinner on the third night Cheryl announced, "I'm going back to work tomorrow." She had decided. It wasn't a discussion point.

Eddie's eyes showed the concern of a loving husband. He laid his hand on hers. "Don't you think it's too early?"

Cheryl smiled briefly. "No, I think it will help."

"No, Mommy, stay home," Mitch giggled.

Eddie squeezed her hand. "Yeah, you tell her, Mitch! Mommy, stay home."

"Mommy, stay home!" Ronnie chimed, shouting home as if his little life depended on it.

Vinh remained silent, staring at the food on his plate.

Cheryl stood and started clearing dishes from the table.

"Boys, as much as I love you all, Mommy's going back to work."

Deep down, Eddie hoped that Cheryl going back to work would begin the healing process, as painful as that might be for her. He wished for her to leave the nightmare behind and return her brand of joy, laughter, and humor to the rest of the grieving family.

•

Once the dishes were done and the boys in bed, Cheryl and Eddie readied themselves for bed in silence. He couldn't find a way to get her to talk about what happened—he didn't know how to.

Later, Eddie lay there in bed with his eyes open, unable to close them.

He understood he couldn't stop what was coming, but whatever it was, it would change his life forever.

Change or die was the way he'd lived in 'Nam.

The dread he felt wouldn't allow his eyes to close; it had his stomach churning. He knew he couldn't reverse what was going to happen, so his only choice was to embrace it. Eddie believed that when fear went away, it meant he was in control of the situation.

He drifted off eventually, headed for another restless, dream-filled sleep.

•

She cried out, "No, not my baby." Eddie felt Cheryl roll over hard on the bed, waking him.

She rolled again, drawing her body in tight, arms and knees protecting her stomach.

"Don't you hurt my Ray," she growled.

Eddie reached over, pulling her into him. Now, after all these years of her saving him from his nightmares, it was his turn to return the favor.

He felt her sweat-soaked nightgown sticking against her hot skin. He held her tight. "I got you, you're okay, Cheryl. I have you."

He used the same kind words she always used on him.

They seemed to work. She relaxed in his arms.

"You're safe now."

She began to cry as she moved her cheek against his. "It's not fair."

They fell back to sleep, holding each other.

•

A half an hour passed before Cheryl slowly extracted herself from Eddie's too-hot embrace and rolled to her side of the bed. It woke Eddie. He wouldn't be able to get back to sleep, and it was pointless trying.

He wandered to the living room and sat in the overstuffed swivel chair, which he turned to face the front window. His pistol lay on his lap while his hand gently rubbed along the barrel.

He remembered pulling guard duty in the jungles of 'Nam, but this was far worse. It wasn't his buddies that he watched over these days—although one buddy, Vinh, was there, of course. It was his family, his wife and children, that he needed to protect with every last breath in his body.

He wished Dang would walk through the front door.

The gun was poised, and his mind set on revenge.

CHAPTER 15

NEED SOME HELP

Several months after Cheryl came home from the hospital, Eddie and Vinh returned from one of their evening workouts laughing and joking as they entered through the front door. Vinh lightly punched Eddie on the shoulder as they headed to the kitchen.

Eddie saw Cheryl sitting on the sofa, wiping away tears. "What's wrong?"

He reached down and pulled her into an embrace.

She handed him a Zippo cigarette lighter without saying a word.

He tilted his head quizzically as he took it. "Whose is it?"

"Just look and see," Cheryl muttered.

He held the lighter, rotating it around in his hand. It looked and felt familiar. Eddie noted the 23rd Infantry "American" Division emblem on one side and the inscription, "Property of Eddie Henderson," along with a peace sign engraved above the writing on the other side.

"Goddamn it, no!" Eddie held the lighter out. "How did you get this?"

Cheryl placed her head on his shoulder and whimpered, "I found Mitch playing with it. He said a man gave it to him and told him to give it to you. That you lost it."

Eddie stared at the lighter, anger pulsing through his body as he pictured Dang or one of his men talking to his boys.

"Son of a bitch."

"Shh, be quiet." Cheryl glanced down the hall. "We don't want to wake the children."

Eddie flipped the lighter over and over in his hand. "Dang enjoys messing with me more than hurting me." He clenched his fist and walked to the living room window. "Have you seen anyone?" He pulled aside the curtains to look in both directions along the quiet neighborhood street. "Any strange cars stopping near the house?"

"No, I haven't. How could Dang do this to us?" Cheryl cried, breaking down. "How can one man be so cruel?"

He pulled Cheryl in tight, attempting to smother her fear.

•

Several evenings later, Eddie decided to contact some old friends. He wasn't going to forget about Dang or the man with the bamboo stick. The memory of that night replayed constantly. But they were going to pay for what they did to his family, to Cheryl and their baby boy, Ray.

"Cheryl, it's time we talk about that night." Eddie wrapped his arms around her waist as she stood at the stove. "You need to know that I'm going to do something about it."

She took a sharp intake of breath as if she could never exhale again.

"What . . . what are you going to do?" Her hand froze with the spoon over the sauce she was heating. "They're dangerous people. Please, we saw last time what they could do to us."

"That's why I need to stop them." He put his chin on her shoulder and whispered, "I need to kill them before they come back."

Cheryl moved the spoon through the sauce in a fast, circular motion, quicker and quicker as she thought about the threat Dang and his men posed to her family. "I want them dead too," she said to his surprise. She stopped stirring to wipe away the tears that streamed down her freckled cheeks. "I want them dead, so maybe . . . someday, you know, we could have another baby and not be scared every minute of our lives. Yes, kill them." She turned and faced her husband. "I didn't think I would ever utter words like that, but I mean it. But this time, you have to know it will work. You have to promise me that will we never, ever be back to living in fear."

He lifted her chin, kissing her lightly on the mouth.

"Killing them is the only solution that will allow us to live in peace."

He licked the salty taste of her tears from his lips.

The dinner table was quiet; everyone appeared deep in thought. While eating, Eddie pictured Dang and the sneer that frequently pulled at his lips. He hadn't missed a detail during the attack on his family; the looks, the words said, and the action taken were the ones that could most destroy him. Those memories would always be with him.

The sight of Dang made him sick to his stomach. He'd forgotten that he could so easily hate, but he knew he'd encountered evil when confronted by the Viet Cong lieutenant and the man with the bamboo stick.

·

After dinner, Eddie rummaged through his army paperwork until he found the envelope that contained addresses and phone numbers. He recalled the day that his buddies had given it to him, along with a carton of Marlboros and a bottle of Jim Beam. It had been a going-away gift before the army shipped him to Japan to recover from his wound.

It was the same day he learned that Dang had escaped from the prisoner-of-war camp in Chu Lai. Eddie felt an inferno inside him that seemed to boil his blood. His face turned red with the bottled-up rage he struggled to hold back. Killing Dang would be so easy. It would come without a second thought, without guilt, free of remorse or what ifs.

Sitting on the edge of the bed, Eddie opened the envelope. He read the names, addresses, and telephone numbers of James Brighton, Carl Johnston, Juan Jackson—known as Little JJ—and Marvin Williams. These were the men he had served with during his last tour.

His first phone call would be to Carl Johnston. The first time he'd met Carl was on the airplane heading to Vietnam for his second tour. A black sergeant sat in the seat next to Eddie's. He had short hair, a square jaw, and clean-shaven face. He was a big man with broad shoulders and muscular arms even though he wasn't much older than Eddie. That was Carl.

Eddie went to the kitchen with the envelope in his hand. He removed the handset from the cradle of the telephone hanging on the wall, holding it to his ear. After he heard a dial tone he deliberately pushed one button after another of the first number. Once his finger pressed the last button, he waited for a connection. There was a moment of silence. While his eyes darted around the room, he heard a ringing sound.

After two rings, a woman answered. "Hello?"

Eddie took a breath. "This is Eddie Henderson, may I speak with Carl?"

"Carl doesn't live here anymore. I'm his mother."

Eddie silently sighed. "Do you have a number where I can reach him?"

"Yes, hang on, and I'll give it to you."

He wrote the telephone number down. "Thank you, Mrs. Johnston, I appreciate it."

He hung up and immediately dialed the number she had given him.

"Action Security, how can I help you?" a man answered.

Startled that it was a business, Eddie hesitated and then asked, "Can I speak to Carl Johnston?"

"This is Johnston—how can I help?"

Eddie smiled. "Damn, Carl, don't you recognize my voice?"

The line was silent for a moment. "Eddie Henderson, I'll be damned. How are you? It's been too long."

"About ten years to be exact," Eddie replied.

"Has it been that long?" Carl asked. "And you've been missing me all this time?"

Eddie laughed, taking a seat at the kitchen table. "You own a private security company? That's impressive. Guess I should have done something like that."

"Yeah, well, it's not so glam. Not here anyway, looking after primped-up celebs and their phony lifestyles, mostly. It ain't on a par with 'Nam, that's for sure, but it pays the bills. So what's up, buddy?"

Eddie shifted in his chair. "I live in Austin, Texas, and I found Dang."

Carl was silent for a moment. "I'll be damned. So, what happened?"

"It's a long story. But Dang killed my son, Ray, and he hurt my wife, Cheryl." Eddie moved to the kitchen window and pushed the curtains open.

Carl was quiet. "I don't know what to say, man . . . Hell, I'm sorry about your son. It can't be easy for you both. How is your wife doing?"

"Thanks, Carl. Well, she's doing the best she can. Hopefully, we'll be able to move forward from this. But I can't do it on my own."

"So, this is what the call is about, I would guess?" Carl asked. "What do you need me to do?"

"I need some help out here." Eddie stared at the million stars that shone brightly in the sky. "I know it's a big ask. You can tell me to fuck off."

"Shit, why would I do that? Listen, I'm all in. Let me get my schedule cleared. I'll be out in a couple of days."

Eddie rubbed his jaw.

"I'm grateful and everything, but you don't need to come right away. I'm thinking in December, during my school break. That will give us time to come up with a workable plan. That work for you?"

"You got it. Let's stay in touch during that time. You know, doing this job, I have contacts everywhere. I'll be ready when you give the go-ahead," Carl said. "And if we need more men, I can get them. Just say what's needed and I'll put it together. Fuck me, man. Dang's gotta go."

"You don't know how much I appreciate it." Eddie's eyes followed a falling star. It might have seemed like a sign if he remotely believed in all that shit.

Carl was going to come through again. He knew it.

It was Carl who had saved him when he'd lain helpless with a wound to the stomach. Eddie recollected a foot crushing Dang's hand, forcing the gun from his grasp before Dang could shoot Eddie in the head.

He'd looked up and seen Carl standing over Dang with his hot M-16 muzzle pressed tight against his temple . . .

"Who else are you calling?" Carl asked.

"I'm going to call Marvin Williams and Little JJ." Eddie picked up the card.

"I'm guessin' you didn't hear about Williams, then?" Carl asked.

Eddie ran his hand through his hair. "No, what happened? Did he get hurt after I left?"

"No, not in 'Nam. I called to offer him a job two years ago. His wife told me he'd topped himself. You know, committed suicide."

The shock made Eddie pause. He remembered Williams as an asset to the squad when he'd come in to replace Cain.

He fit right in and pulled his weight, a good soldier. A story that Marvin told about going to Woodstock always made him smile.

Eddie's eyes narrowed. "No way, not Marvin."

"Yeah, I know. Fucked up, isn't it?" Carl muttered. "I wonder how many veterans can't adjust and call it quits? Maybe that's partly why I do what I do. Can't put the guns down, and I need a team around me."

"I get that, but I can't believe Marvin would end his life."

"I know." Carl's voice faded.

There was a moment of silence between the two men.

"You got anything else?" Carl asked.

Eddie rubbed his jaw. "No, not right now. I'll be calling again soon."

"Okay, talk to you later. Look me up anytime. Now you know where I am." The phone went quiet; Carl had ended the call.

Eddie stood at the window, absentmindedly holding the handset to his ear while watching the night sky. He woke from his daze, pressed the telephone cradle, and released it to receive a dial tone.

He dialed the San Antonio number of Juan Jackson. Eddie smiled while the phone rang. This guy's nickname was Little JJ because of his initials and his small stature. He stood five feet even and weighed less than one hundred thirty pounds. Juan had a Hispanic accent and used that to his advantage at times. He loved to make the guys laugh by goofing around, especially with Bear.

"Hello," a male voice answered.

"Eddie Henderson, calling for Juan . . . Little JJ."

Eddie felt the anticipation building.

"Well shit, Eddie Henderson. This is Juan."

Eddie smiled. "How you been, Little JJ?"

He hesitated. "How about calling me Juan from now on? The name Little JJ reminds me of Bear."

"I can do that, no problem." Eddie's eyes glistened.

David Russel had been a huge man with broad shoulders and thick, bristly tree-trunk legs. The squad soon nicknamed him Bear because of his size and the hair that covered every inch of skin. And like a grizzly, he had a temper.

The image of two VC jumping Bear came back to Eddie. He recalled that Bear easily shook them off his massive frame then killed both of them, even shooting another enemy soldier running away. Then Bear's head exploded as he fell to the ground. Eddie remembered him lying with open eyes, blankly staring at the sky with half his skull missing. Dang had killed him.

"Thanks," Juan said. "Anyway, to answer your question, you know how it is for Vietnam veterans. It's been fucking hard. I can't keep a job, and it's still tough to find someone willing to hire a vet." The line was silent for a moment. "I know some of it is my fault. I tend to drink a bit too much. Got married twice, but neither one lasted. And that was because of my drinking too, so they said." Another pause from Juan. "No children. As I said, it's been fucking hard." He laughed. "Hell, I live with my mother."

"I'm sorry you're having a hard time. Maybe it's not the best time to ask for help."

Eddie stretched the phone cord to the sink and filled a glass with water.

"No, it's probably a good time," Juan said.

Eddie sat in the chair. "I'm your neighbor. I moved to Austin not long ago."

Juan laughed. "Shit, we're only seventy-five miles apart. We need to get together soon then, don't we?"

"Yes, we do. Apologize for not calling sooner." Eddie reached for the glass and took a sip.

"I'm sorry. I got sidetracked. What was it you needed again?" Juan asked.

"Well, I haven't told you yet why I was calling. But . . ." Eddie twisted the cord in his fingers. Then he blurted out, "I found Dang."

Juan was silent, and then muttered, "So, what happened? You okay? Are you in jail or something?"

"I'm not in jail, but I soon might be. I need your help. I need to kill Dang." He stared out the open window at the moon that shone brightly in the sky. "I know I'm asking a lot from you. It's okay to say no."

He thought he'd try the same line he'd said to Carl.

"You can tell me to fuck the hell off." Eddie dug his sharp nails into his palm, anxious that Juan would say no. He needn't have worried.

"Man, I'm all in. That son of a bitch killed Bear. I'd give anything to take his ass out!" Juan yelled. "When do you need me? Just say the word and I'm there."

Eddie turned his focus back to the phone call. "It'll be in December during my school break. I'll have a plan together by then. Carl Johnston is coming to help too." Eddie chugged the rest of the water.

"That's great. Carl's a good man. Someone you want guarding your back. How's he doing these days?" Juan asked.

"He's doing well." Eddie set the glass down. "I'm excited about the squad getting back together."

"Me too. Give me a call when you're ready." Juan said. "Talk to you later."

The phone line disconnected. Eddie straightened out the tangled phone cord for a few seconds, then placed the handset back into the cradle.

He stood for several minutes doing nothing, replaying the two conversations with his old war brothers. His excitement began to build, not only to see Carl and Juan, but at the thought of killing Dang and the man with the stick.

After he made himself a Jim Beam and Coke, Eddie dialed James Brighton's telephone number. Brighton had been his platoon leader for both tours, and they'd grown close. Eddie respected him.

The phone rang a third time.

"Hello, the Brighton residence," a booming southern voice answered.

"This is Eddie Henderson, how are you doing, LT?"

Eddie took a sip of his drink.

"Well, Eddie Henderson! This is a surprise. Not exactly the voice I was expecting to hear, but a most welcome one, nevertheless."

"Who were you expecting to hear?"

"Anyone but you, Henderson! Anyone but you. But it's great to hear from you. And I'm doing fine. How about you?"

"I'm doing well, LT. Life has been good to me since coming back from 'Nam." Henderson rubbed his chin. "How about you, what did you do when you got back? I believed you of all people would've stayed in the army. As I recall, you couldn't get enough of it back in the day."

"No, I got out. Maybe it was all a front. Had you ever thought of that? Honestly, I couldn't take it anymore," Brighton said. "After the army discharged me, I went into the seminary and several years ago became an ordained minister. I live a quiet and respectable life now. Hard to believe, I know, but there you are. That's how it is.

My wife and I have three children, all girls." Brighton laughed out loud.

After receiving the news of LT being a minister, Eddie didn't want to involve him with his situation. Murder and the ministry didn't mix too well.

"That's great, LT." He smiled. "I have two sons now and we're all living in Austin, Texas. I'm a history teacher. Can you believe that?"

The two combat buddies talked for over an hour, chatting about their two years together in Vietnam and their new lives. Eddie ended the conversation without ever asking him for help. How could he, now that Brighton had revealed himself as a man of God?

Good for him.

He chugged the drink until the ice cubes clinked at the bottom of the glass. Now it was time to make a plan.

Eddie was pouring another drink when Cheryl came up behind him. "Hey." She hugged him. "I want one too. You never made me one?" She put her arms around his neck and kissed his cheek.

He reached for another glass and poured her a drink.

Eddied faced his wife. "Cheryl, so you know, I'm getting a plan together. Revenge is coming."

Cheryl smiled. "Good."

They tapped their glasses together.

THE MAKINGS OF A PLAN

Three to four times a week, Vinh and Eddie went to the gym after Eddie bathed the boys and tucked them into bed. Eddie introduced him to lifting weights and taekwondo, and the trainer worked with Vinh to build some lean muscle on his thin, wiry frame.

The instructor told them that regular training would help burn fat and tone the body. Eddie found that by practicing taekwondo, he'd improved his speed and endurance—and he liked it because this type of fighting involved kicking and self-defense.

Occasionally, after a workout, Eddie would call Carl and Juan to come up with a feasible strategy to find Dang and his men. He suspected they were still in Houston; and better yet, they were probably living in the Little Saigon district. This would reduce their search area, but Eddie knew the residents would be reluctant to give the Americans information about Dang's whereabouts.

One night, Eddie learned that Carl knew a private detective in Houston who owed him a favor. And Carl thought it was high time to call in that favor. There was no time like the present, and no better task than the one they were planning.

Carl gave the detective Dang's full name and description, including his job as the fishermen's union leader. Everyone believed it was a bogus position. There was little doubt among the men that

Dang was probably extorting money from the fishermen, not helping them.

•

Weeks later, after a Friday night phone call with Carl, Eddie opened the kitchen cabinet and pulled down the bottle of Jim Beam. "I need a drink." He glanced at Vinh, who was sitting at the table. "Don't ask. You're too young to drink."

Vinh chuckled. "Oh, come on Eddie, I've earned it by now."

Eddie poured two drinks and handed one to him. "Don't you go and tell Cheryl." He gave Vinh a stern glare that made him smile. "We'd both have hell to pay if she found out I gave you alcohol."

Cheryl strode into the kitchen. "Hell to pay for what?" She looked at Vinh and the drink that set in front of him. "Oh. Right. I see now. I'll have that." She shot Eddie a disapproving glance. "Really?"

Eddie winked at Vinh.

"We had a call from Carl. Looks like his friend is coming through."

"What did he say?" Cheryl looked over the rim of the glass while she took a sip.

"His contact in Houston managed to locate where Dang and his men spend most of their time. They live in one of Houston's poorest communities, Allen Parkway Village, in the shadows of downtown Houston." Eddie picked up his notes. "The detective claimed he found what he called their headquarters, located in an old abandoned warehouse not far from the Little Saigon district. Dang has as many as four men with him most of the time, the guy said."

"Did he have anything else to say?" Cheryl brushed strands of hair away from her face.

Eddie was sure the woman could read his mind. No matter what he told her, she always knew if there was more to say. Female intuition, people called it. He sniggered to himself. *Witchcraft, I say.*

But Cheryl was right, of course. There was more.

"Yeah, he said the fishermen didn't like Dang much, and that they were afraid of him. Just as we thought. Union leader, my ass."

Cheryl sat next to Vinh. "It's not surprising that he has them scared."

Eddie placed a hand on her shoulder. "Well, I've saved the best for last. Vinh and I are going to meet Juan tomorrow. Then the three of us will go to Houston and check it out. We'll verify the detective's information."

Cheryl peered into his eyes. "I wish you would call the police. Dang and his men are horrible people and need to be arrested."

"We've talked about this. I need to take care of Dang for good, and putting him in jail won't help." He licked his dry lips. "We would be doing this all over again when he got out in a few years." He touched her cheek. "Besides, I owe Ray Laurel. I promised him."

"No sense in arguing. But you two be careful." She bit her lower lip while shooting a worried glance. "I mean it."

"We will." Eddie smiled. "We're going to recon the area and get the layout of his headquarters at the warehouse. That's it. No more shenanigans. Not this time. I don't want a repeat encounter."

"Good, and that'd better be all."

Cheryl kissed him on the cheek.

"It's getting late. I'm going to bed." Eddie set his glass down in the sink and Cheryl handed Eddie her glass.

"Me too." She smiled.

"Good night." Vinh pushed his chair in and went to his bedroom.

•

Once the house was quiet and everyone had fallen asleep, a tree branch brushed the roof as the wind picked up during the night. Eddie woke to the sound. He walked into the living room carrying his pistol.

After he determined there were no intruders, Eddie sat in the overstuffed chair that he again had turned to face the living room window.

The tiniest gap in the curtains allowed him to look through to the street outside. His gun was lying on his lap while he stared out at the star-filled night. Every now and then Eddie's eyes closed and his head slumped to his chest. He fought the urge to fall asleep.

•

Cheryl placed her hand gently on his shoulder.

"Eddie, it's time to get up. What are you doing here?"

He opened his eyes and looked at her quizzically.

"I live here." He didn't understand why she would even ask him that.

"No, silly." She shook his shoulder. "What are you doing asleep in the chair?"

"Oh, that! Sorry. It's just that, as usual, I heard some noises last night." He stood and cupped her cheek, kissing her gently on the lips. "I'm going to put this away." He held up the pistol. "Can you start the coffee?"

"I think I can do that. But I wish you wouldn't have the gun out." Cheryl strolled to the kitchen.

When Eddie returned, he found Vinh at the table drinking coffee. The boys were there too, slurping down Fruit Loops as if tomorrow might bring a cereal famine. "Can I have more, Mom?" Mitch whined.

Cheryl ignored him. The boy could eat and eat, and it wasn't healthy.

"Here's your breakfast." Cheryl placed two bowls of oatmeal on the table for Eddie and Vinh.

"Morning to you, too." Eddie poured a cup of coffee. "You ready for the drive?" He glanced at Vinh. "We'll be leaving to meet Juan in thirty minutes."

Vinh took a mouthful of oatmeal. "I'm ready." He held his mouth open, displaying the food.

Mitch and Ronnie laughed and then held their mouths open, showing chewed Fruit Loops.

Cheryl shot Vinh a stern glance. "Thanks for teaching the boys good table manners." She hesitated for a moment. "I'm sorry. I didn't mean to snap. I'm a little on edge."

"It's okay." Vinh stood and hugged Cheryl. "Sometimes I forget. I'm sorry."

"Don't be." She shot Vinh a mother's look. "If they grow up copying you, I won't have much to complain about. You're a good person."

"Thank you, ma'am." Vinh's smile went ear to ear.

•

After breakfast, Vinh and Eddie left the house and got into the car. Cheryl watched them back out and drive off toward the interstate. The two rode in silence.

Within minutes, Eddie turned south onto I-35. They would meet Juan not far from the intersection of I-35 and I-10. There, Eddie would leave his car at the Exxon station and they'd continue the trip in Juan's vehicle.

Once they pulled into the gas station, Eddie parked at a pump. "We might as well fill up while we're here."

"I'm going to get something to munch on," Vinh said over his shoulder as he strolled into the store.

As Eddie watched the digits scroll on the pump, he felt a hand on his shoulder. He jumped back, facing the person while taking an instinctively defensive position.

"Damn, Juan, you scared the shit out of me." Eddie embraced his friend. "Thanks for helping."

Juan stepped back. "Man, no problem. You look great."

To Eddie, Juan hadn't changed too much. His dark hair touched his shoulders and his belly hung over his belt, but generally, he still looked fit enough and had muscular arms.

"Looks like you've been putting away some beer." Eddie chuckled.

"More bourbon than anything else." Juan punched him in the shoulder.

Vinh approached the two friends with arms full of snacks.

"Juan, this is Vinh. You probably remember him. He was at Chu Lai while you were still there."

"Jesus, Vinh, you've grown since the last time I saw you. You're a man now." Juan extended his hand. "Good to see you again, buddy."

After Vinh adjusted the items in his arms, he shook the man's hand. "I remember you, too. And yes, I've grown a bit. I hope I'll be useful to you on our . . . mission."

Eddie placed the nozzle back into the cradle and closed the gas cap. "Let's go. We'll be there in less than two hours." After settling the bill, Eddie parked his vehicle at the far side of the station. "Anyway, I meant to say thanks for taking your car, Juan. They might recognize mine."

Eddie reached under the seat and grabbed the pistol. Once he stepped away from the vehicle, he slid the gun into his waistband.

The three men climbed into Juan's Mazda.

During the drive to Houston, the friends talked of their time in the war. The subject soon changed to what they'd been doing since coming home. Vinh sat quietly and passed around his snacks, like a kid in the back of his parents' car on a nice trip out for the day. Only, this was no nice day out.

Once they got to Houston, Juan followed Eddie's careful directions, taking Bellaire Boulevard and heading toward Little Saigon.

"We should be there soon."

Eddie felt the anticipation tingling through every vein of his body.

The two passengers sat up, staring out the windows as if watching for danger. Juan pulled into a parking spot under the branches of a large oak tree, coasting to a stop.

Eddie surveyed the street and parking lot. "Should keep us out of sight while we check the area out."

Juan glanced at Eddie as he pulled the pistol out from underneath his seat and tucked it into his waistband.

"You got that down to a fine art," Juan said, seeing Eddie twice settle the pistol into his clothing. "You always carry?"

Eddie simply shook his head. Now wasn't the time for talking. "No," was all he managed. Eddie watched Vietnamese refugees ambling along the roadway as if they were still in Vietnam. Some even wore traditional clothing with a conical hat and a pajama-like shirt and pants, along with sandals.

The younger Asians wore blue jeans with brightly colored T-shirts that hung loosely over their bodies. They, too, wore sandals. The sights and smells could've been from any large city in Vietnam.

"Vinh, why don't you walk around the block and see what you can find out from the locals?" He pointed toward the housing projects. "Juan and I will stay on the main road."

"Got it. What if there's a problem?" Vinh asked.

"Meet here at the car." Eddie adjusted his pistol. "Let's meet back here in two hours and compare notes."

The men separated, with Eddie and Juan going in one direction and Vinh in another.

Eddie glared toward the sounds coming from the street—the sing-song voices, the motorcycles zooming along the main road. His need for revenge seemed to creep through every pore in his body. He felt it festering like the jungle rot he'd endured in Vietnam. Eddie knew the only way to get rid of something that festered and stank in the pores was to keep the area clean and rid it of whatever scourge afflicted it.

This was precisely what he planned to do with Dang and his men; he saw it as his task to clean the area of evil, to flush out the vermin and shoot them dead.

•

While Vinh strolled casually along the sidewalk, he stopped and conversed with the locals, making small talk. All the while, he scanned the area, searching for Dang or one of his men.

On one occasion, an elderly Vietnamese man with a long gray beard and traditional clothes stopped and talked to Vinh in Vietnamese. It emerged they had something in common; both were from the Quang Ngai Province. When Vinh asked about Dang, the old man pointed at a small structure and told Vinh that it was the leader of the fishermen union's headquarters. Music to Vinh's ears. He memorized the location.

Vinh made eye contact. "So, you know *Bảo Đặng?*"

The older man's weathered face flushed as he nervously glanced around the sidewalk, looking this way and that, scanning rooftops and tiny balconies. It was as if the man believed every insect, every tree, and every bird might be listening for his answer. He gave it slowly, cautiously and in a low voice. "I don't know him well. But I do know . . ." He moved in closer, so he could lower his voice even more. " . . . I know that the people who live in Little Saigon don't like him." His gaze shifted back to Vinh. "He is cruel and takes our money."

"Does he force the fishermen to pay him?" Vinh asked.

Again, the elderly man scanned the area. "He does. He calls it insurance. But if they don't pay, something happens to their boat. You know what I mean?"

The man stared past Vinh with a look of fear. He bowed slightly and shuffled off without saying a word more, leaving Vinh standing on the sidewalk with so many questions still on the tip of his tongue.

Soon after the older man left, Vinh felt a heavy hand come down on his shoulder. The fingers clamped around his skinny frame like a vice. He stepped forward and tried to spin around to see who it was.

At first, he thought maybe the old man had come back to talk to him further, but then he realized the grip was way too firm. The grip hurt. He reached up with his fingers to try and release the stranger's grasp as he took his first good, long look at the man's face. Horror . . .

"*Tôi biết bạn,*" the heavyset man said. *I know you.*

Vinh immediately recognized the man as the one he'd shot. The man's bulky, useless left arm hung at his side.

"No, you don't know me." Vinh's heartbeat said otherwise.

Vinh shifted his feet for a better defensive stance.

"Yes, I know you." The man moved his right hand toward his waistband. "You shot me. Like this . . ."

The man raised his arm, the forefinger and middle finger pulled together like a handgun. "Bang, bang!"

And now he moved again for the weapon at his waist, taunting Vinh.

In one motion, Vinh swiveled on the ball of his left foot, and with his right leg, delivered a spinning hook kick. His foot connected so hard to the man's face that blood spurted out of his mouth, along with several already chipped and misshapen teeth. The man hit the ground hard.

Vinh stood over him as he moaned.

When the man struggled to get to his feet, Vinh stamped down on his left shoulder, grinding his heel into where the wound must be. The man yelled in pain. Noticing a gathering crowd, Vinh sprinted off to where Juan had parked the car. He didn't look back.

•

Eddie and Juan sat in a restaurant across the street from the warehouse. From their window seat, they intently watched people come and go from the building.

"I can't believe the number of white, black, and Mexican people that are walking the streets and shopping here in Little Saigon." Eddie leaned forward in his chair for a better view of the sidewalk.

Juan gazed out the window. "I have to say, I'm surprised too. This would be the last place I would come to shop or eat. You know, given a choice, I mean." He turned in his chair to face Eddie. "Brings back too many bad memories."

"Yeah, it does." Eddie clenched his fist. "Way too many."

Eddie took notes of what he observed. On occasion, Juan would lean close and whisper information for him to write down.

He also drew a detailed sketch of the building, including windows, doors, and the immediate surrounding area. The warehouse was roughly two hundred feet long and fifty feet wide. It appeared to be a prefab building with tan metal siding and a tin roof that hung over the walls about eight inches. Eddie noticed the front door with a window facing the street and a windowless side door about one hundred and twenty-five feet from the front of the building. The side door faced a row of bushes and a driveway for the adjacent house.

A sidewalk went from the street to the front door, and there was a massive live oak tree with heavy limbs hanging close to the ground about forty feet from the front door.

"Next time, we'll bring a camera," Eddie muttered. "I can't believe I left it on the kitchen counter. After all that prep, too."

Juan took his eyes off the building to glance at Eddie. He figured he was talking to himself.

A young pretty Vietnamese woman stopped at the table.

"Do you want another beer?"

She pushed her long dark hair back as she picked up the empty bottles. Eddie was a little surprised that she wore the traditional *áo dài*, a tunic over pants. Hers was white with black silk-like pants.

Eddie turned the writing tablet over and laid it on the table face down.

Juan glanced at Eddie. "Sure, bring us two more. Why not?"

Once she left to fetch the beer, Eddie looked around the room. "I haven't seen a sign of Dang, have you?"

"No, I haven't." Juan wiped the sweat from his brow. "Nothing unusual, either."

The waitress returned with the two beverages.

"You need anything else?"

Juan smiled and took a swig from the beer bottle. "No thanks." He took a drink from his flask and washed the bourbon down with half the beer, as if time was due to run out and the world about to end.

"Come on, slow down." Eddie grabbed Juan's arm. "That's enough."

Juan jerked his arm away. "Don't worry about me." He took another drink of his beer. "I'm fine."

Eddie shook his head and picked up his beer bottle. While taking a long drink, he watched the side door. "Damn." He set the bottle down hard, making a smacking sound. The customers fell quiet. After a minute, they began talking and eating.

Juan set his drink down. "What's wrong?"

"Red Cadillac, over there, parked in front of the warehouse. The man with the bamboo stick was driving. And I swear I saw Dang and a woman, roughly his age and holding onto his arm, walk into the building." Eddie ran his hand through his hair. "I bet it's that son of a bitch's wife."

"You gotta be kidding me." Juan laughed, the alcohol already taking effect. "Who would marry that bastard?"

Eddie's eyes went wide. "I wonder if she knows that he killed her son?" He lifted the bottle. "I bet she doesn't."

Juan smiled and tilted his head to the side. "Well, now we know this is their headquarters, or whatever you want to call it."

"Let's go back to the car. Vinh should be there by now." Eddie threw a ten-dollar bill on the table as he stood.

Juan pushed his chair out. "That's a generous tip." He took another sip from the flask.

Eddie looked at Juan as if it was the first time. "I'm starting to worry about your drinking." He laid his hand on Juan's shoulder, unable to keep the concern out of either his eyes or his voice. "I know things have been hard since we got back from 'Nam, but I need you. The team needs you." He squeezed Juan's shoulder and then dropped his hand. He hoped his words calmed Juan. The last thing he needed was for Juan to be drunk when the shit hit the fan.

"Don't worry about me." Juan smiled and punched Eddie in the arm. "I'll be there when you need me." But his slurred speech and slightly wavering gait said otherwise.

Bad idea to bring Juan, Eddie thought. *A fucking bad idea.*

The two men strolled through the doorway at the same time as a large Asian man dressed in a suit without a tie bumped into them. He gave them a hard stare. "Watch where you're going."

Eddie smiled. "Excuse us." They stepped through the doorway onto the sidewalk, heading for the car.

Once they reached it, it took only a second for Vinh to step out from behind the thick tree trunk. "It's about time. Let me in, quick."

Juan unlocked the car and Vinh piled into the back seat, ducking down.

"What, did something happen?" Eddie asked as he and Juan stood by the open door. "From the look of you, I'm guessing it's a yes." He stared at Vinh. "You okay?"

"Yeah, I'm fine, thanks to the taekwondo training." Vinh chuckled now. "I had to use that spinning kick. I knew it'd be useful someday." He took a breath and hesitated. "It was the man I shot at the house."

"Damn, they must all be here, then." Eddie scanned the street that ran in front of the parking area. "Glad you're okay."

Juan placed a hand on Vinh's shoulder. "You're a badass!"

Everyone laughed

Eddie snatched the car keys from Juan. "I'm driving." He slid behind the wheel as Juan fell into the passenger seat without saying a word.

The car sped off.

•

On the trip along I-10 back to the gas station where Eddie left his car, the three men strategized, finally confirming that the Christmas break would be the perfect time to hit Dang.

Eddie concluded it was a good idea to call Carl again. Then he'd ask Carl's detective to take pictures of the warehouse and the union office and anyone that seemed to be associated with Dang. The guy could mail the photographs to Eddie. Dang and his men didn't know the detective, so he should be able to take the pictures without drawing attention.

He wanted to keep the plan simple and not hurt any civilians. For Eddie, the objective was Dang and the man with the bamboo stick, Canh.

MERRY CHRISTMAS TO ALL

After eating Thanksgiving dinner, the family gathered in the living room. The children sat near the tree, talking about what Santa Claus would bring them. Vinh sat next to the boys on the floor, encouraging them to show him where Saint Nick should put their gifts.

Eddie plugged in the Christmas lights. The boys got more excited about Santa coming as the lights twinkled, reflecting different colors from the decorations.

"Daddy, this is my ornament." Mitch held up an ornament of Santa on a sleigh.

Ronnie ran to Cheryl carrying a large red ball with his name on it. "This is mine, Mommy."

Cheryl picked Ronnie up into her lap. "Let's go shopping at Highland mall tomorrow."

"Good idea. But it will be crowded." Eddie frowned.

Cheryl squeezed his hand. "You're a big boy, you can handle it." She smiled. "Right, Ronnie?"

"Daddy, a big boy!" Ronnie yelled, and then he giggled.

•

After breakfast the next morning the family piled into the sedan. Vinh sat between the boys, making sure they buckled their seat belts. Eddie started the car, wheeling out of the driveway and heading toward the mall.

He looked in the rearview mirror and noticed an older car had pulled onto the street after he backed out.

He knew that observing the car made him more anxious; he felt the tension building behind his eyes. Eddie needed to shake it off.

His fingers curled into Cheryl's hand as he turned her way with a smile, hoping not to give away that he was worried.

She smiled back, her face beaming.

The drive took about fifteen minutes, and Eddie kept checking the mirror. Sure enough, the same car stayed roughly three cars behind him.

Intentionally, he drove around the parking lot as if looking for a parking space for five minutes. The car appeared to hold back while Eddie searched the lot. He decided to park as close to the entrance as possible.

Once the car coasted into the spot, he turned the ignition off while opening the car door. Eddie stood watching the vehicle as it parked several rows away. *Damn, am I getting paranoid or what?*

Cheryl helped Vinh get the boys out of the back seat, and the family entered the mall holding hands. Once inside, Eddie pulled Vinh aside.

Eddie looked around. "I think we're being followed."

Vinh nodded in affirmation.

"Cheryl, why don't you and the boys go ahead, and we'll meet you at the toy store." Eddie kissed her on the cheek.

"Is something wrong?" Cheryl asked.

"I don't know. Go on to the store. We'll be there shortly." Eddie's eyes surveyed the entrance as Cheryl walked toward the toy store.

The men strolled to the information sign and stood on the opposite side of the doorway. Both had a clear view of the entrance with some concealment from the sign.

Within minutes, two Vietnamese men sporting short-cropped hair and suits without ties entered the mall. They stood at the entrance, talking as they scanned the area.

Eddie nudged Vinh. "Can you make out what they're saying?"

"No, not a word." Vinh shook his head. "They're too far away."

"You stay here, and I'll see if they follow me." Eddie peeked around the sign. "Follow them if they do." He stepped out into the walkway in full view of the two men. The taller one now pointed in Eddie's direction. The two Vietnamese men followed Eddie as he strolled through the crowd.

Vinh waited until they were a distance down the walkway then started to follow them.

Up ahead, Eddie stopped and peered into a store window. He took a casual glance behind him and spotted the two men. They stood stationary, too. After a minute, Eddie wandered down the crowded walkway until he reached a service door. He entered and took long strides along the hallway. Once he turned the corner, he stopped with his back against the wall.

As he waited, the adrenaline began pumping through his body. He thought of running away to save himself, but he remained frozen to the spot. Eddie understood that he had two choices: to flee and abandon his family and Vinh, or stay and fight. His throat was dry and sweat ran down his face. He knew there was nothing more important than his family. He felt guilty to even think of running.

The two men followed, unaware of Vinh a short distance behind them. They talked to each other as they took quick strides.

Their focus was on Eddie.

He settled in for the wait, but it was only moments before the man in front turned the corner to catch up with him. Eddie stayed still while his panic faded away. Neither man said a word.

Once the man stepped forward, he saw Eddie and threw a left-handed roundhouse punch at the side of his head. Eddie, sensing the punch was coming, ducked under the blow. It barely missed; he felt the man's fist go skimming through his hair.

The man's fist slammed into the concrete wall with his full body weight behind the punch. He grunted in pain, dropping his hand to his side.

After he ducked, Eddie regained his balance on the balls of his feet. He clenched his right hand and swung a spinning backfist into the face of the tall Vietnamese man. The back of his hand made contact, and his momentum carried a powerful knockout punch. Eddie heard the bone crunch when he pulled his fist away.

The man crumpled to the floor.

When Vinh's sneakers squeaked on the freshly waxed tile floor, the second man turned to face him. Vinh extended his right leg to the left side of the target. While at full-extension, his foot snapped to the side, impacting the stalker with the heel of his foot. His head snapped back, slamming into the concrete wall from the force of the blow.

The man shook his head as he stood straighter, then he took up a fighting stance while Vinh circled to his left.

His lips curled into a snarl as he stepped toward Vinh.

Eddie rounded the corner.

The man quickly turned in Eddie's direction with a surprised look.

Before he could defend himself, Eddie delivered a right upper-cut to his opponent's chin. The sound of teeth breaking echoed in the hall. The smaller man slid to the floor unconscious, his mouth dripping blood and teeth as he went down.

Eddie looked along the corridor. "Let's get the hell out of here."

They left the two Vietnamese men lying on the floor as they went through the service entrance into the mall.

"This isn't good." Eddie rubbed his knuckles. "I bet they've been watching us all along."

Vinh quickened his pace. "I heard some of their conversation."

"What did they say?" Eddie slowed so Vinh could walk along-side him.

Vinh grabbed Eddie's arm. "The shorter guy said they were going to capture you. Not kill you."

Eddie glanced over his shoulder. "Shit, let's get the hell out of here."

They quickened their pace to the toy store to find Cheryl and the boys.

Once inside, Eddie put his arm around Cheryl's waist. "We need to leave now. A couple of Dang's men are here."

Cheryl faced him. "You sure?"

"Yes." Eddie pulled her toward him.

She didn't protest. Cheryl grabbed the hand of each boy and they walked quickly to the car.

Eddie stopped several parking spots away from his car. "Wait here."

He approached the Fairmont with caution. Eddie lowered himself to the ground and looked underneath the car. Next, he popped the hood open. Once he scanned the motor area, he dropped the hood. "Okay, it's clear."

Eddie got the boys situated into the back seat while Cheryl slid into the front.

After he buckled the boys in, Eddie handed Vinh a pocketknife.

"Go take care of a tire."

"You got it." Vinh strolled to the car.

As he stood waiting, the reasons he needed to kill Dang flooded to him all at once. He felt panic seize him when he recalled how Dang had hurt his wife and killed his son. And then the fear faded when he thought about how he would kill Dang. It had been a long time coming, but now it was time. Things had a habit of coming full circle, some people said. Many called it karma.

Well, whatever it was, it would soon be Dang's turn.

Eddie slowed his breathing to let his thoughts of Cheryl calm him.

After Vinh returned, he climbed in the back seat between the two boys. Eddie started the car for the trip home. He reached for Cheryl's hand as he backed the car out of the parking spot.

•

It was a week from Christmas break, and Eddie's excitement to execute the plan was building inside him. Cheryl's college break would start a week earlier than his holiday, and he hoped that two-and-a-half weeks would be enough time to find and kill Dang.

Once the school bell rang that Friday, Eddie and Vinh picked up the boys and drove home. Vinh jumped from the car to escort Mitch and Ronnie into the house. Before he closed the front door behind them all, Vinh looked over his shoulder, giving a quick wave goodbye.

Eddie backed out of the driveway again, heading to the Austin airport. John and Martha Drexler's flight would arrive soon; it was customary for Mitch's parents to visit the week before the Christmas break.

The boys wouldn't go to daycare; instead they'd spend quality time with Grandma and Grandpa while Eddie finished up the last week at school before the break.

This holiday visit would be the first time that Cheryl would be home with them. Eddie believed it might help her, being around Martha and John. Of course, they told them about Ray, but not about Dang and his men. At the end of the week, they would celebrate Christmas before the grandparents flew back to Indianapolis.

When he drove into the arrival area, Eddie spotted John and Martha standing next to their luggage. He steered the car alongside the curb and stopped. Once his feet hit the ground, he headed straight toward them.

Eddie walked into Martha's embrace. "Oh, Eddie, you look good." She pushed him back to get a better look at him. "I bet you put on some weight."

"Not much weight, I've been exercising. I'm—what's the word—solid now." Eddie grinned. "I think that's what you meant."

John reached for Eddie's hand and gripped it with a firm grasp. "You do look good."

"Thanks, John." Eddie released his hand from John's. "The boys and Cheryl are excited to see you. We do love your visits."

"We wouldn't miss spending time with our grandchildren." Martha grabbed her bag. "Oh my, you and Cheryl, too." She giggled at her error.

Once the car was loaded, Eddie drove toward the house.

Martha leaned forward in the seat. "Eddie, I'm so sorry about Ray. I hope Cheryl is doing better."

"Thanks, she's doing well." Eddie's eyes flickered with sadness.

The rest of the trip was quiet. While glancing at John and Martha, Eddie recalled yet again how he and their son Mitch had gone through training together. He'd even stayed with them while they were on leave before reporting to Vietnam.

His mind flashed to the night his best friend, Mitch Drexler, died in his arms. It was as if it had happened yesterday; he saw the enemy rushing their bunker firing AK-47s, throwing grenades— then the satchel charge that exploded, killing his friend. He held Mitch as the life drained from his body. Eddie recalled the promise he made before Mitch died—the promise he didn't keep. He wiped at his wet eyes.

After Eddie pulled into the driveway, the boys ran toward the car, yelling, "Grandma! Grandpa!"

Within minutes, the family was in the house. Little Mitch was in Grandpa's lap, and Ronnie sat with Grandma.

Eddie looked up as Vinh entered the room.

"John, Martha, this is Vinh. We told you about him."

Martha stood and held her arms out for a hug. Vinh seemed a little confused but moved into her embrace when Eddie nodded his head.

John put an arm around Martha and Vinh. "Welcome to the family."

Vinh flashed a happy smile. "Thank you."

Grandma turned to see the Christmas tree in the far corner of the living room. "Oh my, what a beautiful tree you have, Mitch and Ronnie."

Mitch ran to the tree. "Look at all the presents, Grandma."

"This one is mine!" Ronnie yelled. "You can't have it!"

Ronnie clutched a gift to his chest, possessively.

"Oh, Ronnie, can't Grandma have it?" Martha asked, gently teasing and leaning forward as if she was going to take the foil-wrapped present.

"C'mon, give it to Grandma . . ."

"No!"

Everyone laughed.

Eddie smiled as he watched Martha and the boys interact. To him the scene was perfect. Shiny ornaments adorned the tree, trinkets that the boys had each picked out and hung. The lights glowed on the tree, and there was an aroma of pine in the air. Underneath, there were many presents wrapped in joyful Christmas colors.

Cheryl walked into the room. "Merry Christmas! Now let's eat dinner." She laughed and waved for the family to sit at the table.

•

Four days after the Drexlers arrived, Eddie came home from work excited that the Christmas break was almost here. When he entered through the front door, he saw Cheryl sitting on the sofa, wiping her tears. He heard laughter coming from the boys' bedroom while they played with their grandparents.

Eddie sat next to his wife, putting an arm around her shoulders. "What's wrong?"

She handed him an envelope without saying a word.

He reached inside and removed a Christmas card. The front had a decorated Christmas tree with many presents underneath. The caption read, "Merry Christmas."

Eddie flipped the card open.

"Damn it, no!" He read the writing at the bottom, "Best Wishes to your family. You're still on my list and Santa is watching."

"How could they?" Cheryl placed her head on his shoulder and whimpered. "How could they?"

After staring at the Christmas card, Eddie squeezed her shoulder. "Son of a bitch. I've got to kill them."

"Shh, be quiet. We don't want John and Martha to know." Cheryl looked down the hall.

He pulled Cheryl in close, wanting to protect her. "It will be okay."

"How could Dang do this to us?" Cheryl cried, starting to break down. "And it's Christmas!"

He pulled Cheryl to her feet. "Alright, let's take a deep breath." Eddie breathed in slowly and then exhaled. "You and the boys are heading to Berkeley for your parents Saturday, the day after John and Martha leave." After he pulled her in closer against his body, he whispered, "You and the boys will be safe, and I'll finish the plan. Dang will no longer be a threat to our family."

Cheryl pressed her body into her husband. "Oh, I hope so. I can't live like this much longer."

"Cheryl." Martha walked along the hallway. "Cheryl?"

She wiped her eyes. "We're in the living room."

Martha's face flushed. "Oh my, am I interrupting something?"

Eddie smiled as he released Cheryl. "No, not at all. What's up?"

"Yes, Martha, are you hungry? I can make a quick snack." Cheryl headed for the kitchen.

"Well, yes, that would be nice, dear." She sat on the sofa. "What time are we opening presents tomorrow morning? I assume it will be early because our flight leaves at noon."

Eddie flopped next to Martha. "How about eight o'clock, and then we can have a big breakfast before going to the airport?" He gave her a gentle hug.

•

The same night the Drexlers left to go home, Eddie and Cheryl put the boys to bed and decided it would be good for them to get to bed early too. Cheryl and the kids would leave in the morning for her parents' home during the Christmas break.

Before Eddie turned off the lamp, he reached into the nightstand drawer and removed a manila envelope. "I have something to show you." He slid out a photograph and handed it to Cheryl.

"I got this after that car blew up in the school parking lot."

Her eyes focused on the picture, and she saw the burning car.

There was writing on the bottom edge, and she read, "Missed this time. Next, we won't." She dropped the photograph and cried, "Why didn't you show me this earlier?"

Eddie averted her stern glare. "I assumed I was protecting you. It won't happen again." He gazed into her sad eyes. "From now on, I'll share everything with you."

"You'd better." Cheryl handed him the picture. "I need to know what's going on." She rolled on her side, facing away from him. "Now, turn the lamp off."

•

Early in the morning, Eddie tossed and rolled as if running through the jungle.

He whimpered in his sleep. "Ray, follow me!" Eddie flipped onto his stomach and crawled toward the foot of the bed. "Let's go, Ray!"

"Eddie, it's okay. It's a dream. I have you. You're safe."

Curling up next to him, she murmured, "It's okay. I'm with you now."

•

Eddie had still slept little when the sun streamed through the opening in the bedroom curtain. "Alright, I'm getting up." He reached for Cheryl and discovered her side of the bed was empty.

Eddie felt a sense of panic.

"Cheryl?"

He jumped from the bed and went down the hallway, all the while looking for intruders.

"Cheryl?"

"I'm in here," Cheryl called from the kitchen.

When he saw her standing over the stove, turning pancakes, he smiled. "You're so beautiful when you cook." His arms circled her waist as he put his cheek against hers, taking in her aroma.

She was as pretty as the first day he'd met her. He didn't know what he would do without the sound of her voice or the touch of her skin. His chest ached with the thought of losing her.

"Okay, enough of that, fella," Cheryl giggled. "Go wake the boys."

After breakfast, Cheryl packed while Eddie and Vinh washed the dishes. Once she finished, they carried the luggage to the car.

Eddie kissed Cheryl. "The car is packed."

Vinh sat between Mitch and Ronnie and entertained them on the drive to the airport. Cheryl held Eddie's hand and squeezed it every couple of seconds.

She turned the radio on and a song blared:

"*Where have all the flowers gone . . .*"

"Oh, not that song." Cheryl started crying. She turned the radio off. "Please be careful and don't do anything foolish." She squeezed his hand hard. "Call me every day, promise?"

"I give you my word." Eddie glanced at Cheryl, turning on his boyish grin. "You and the boys will be safe again when you come home. That I promise."

Once the car was parked, the family made their way to the ticket counter. Eddie checked the bags. "Let's go to the gate."

He took Cheryl's arm with one hand and Ronnie's hand in the other. Cheryl took hold of Mitch's little hand as they walked to the gate. Vinh made jokes with Mitch when they stepped onto the moving walkway.

After they got to the departure gate, Eddie thought he sensed that everyone seemed to relax—but he couldn't keep from thinking about Dang.

Eddie couldn't help but think that Dang's men might be waiting at the airport. His eyes scanned each person in the waiting area, and he checked the passengers strolling by to see if they might pose a threat to his family. Eddie wanted to make sure that they didn't follow Cheryl to Berkeley.

He didn't know if it was fear that he felt when thinking about Dang, or anger caused by the rage that lay below the surface. Eddie understood that when he felt frightened, his first reaction was to strike out.

He took a breath, not wanting those feelings to destroy him. He needed to remain calm if he was going to defeat Dang.

When the gate attendant announced the flight was ready to board, he embraced Cheryl. "I love you. Keep an eye out just in case." Next, Eddie gave Mitch and Ronnie hugs and kisses until they yelled for him to stop.

Vinh walked into Cheryl's arms and hugged her hard. "I'll miss you. Take good care of my two brothers." He chuckled.

Cheryl's face took on a concerned look as her eyes welled up.

"Please watch out for Eddie." She stepped back, wiping at the tears. "Don't let him get hurt."

"I will watch him." Vinh dropped his gaze to the floor. "I promise."

"Okay, you two." Eddie slid his hand around her elbow and gently began to steer her as if she was a fragile old lady crossing a busy road.

"It's time to board." His lips turned downward. "Boy, I'll miss you."

He walked his family to the ramp and paused at the doorway. Eddie turned his gaze to Cheryl and then the boys. He knew he would have to let them go, but in his mind, this gave him a couple more moments to be with them. He smiled and then let his family leave, watching them disappear into the airplane.

Eddie turned toward Vinh. "You ready to do this?"

Vinh smiled grimly. "Yes."

The two men walked through the airport toward the car. They had a mission to complete.

THE REUNION

When Eddie pulled into the driveway, he spotted a white van parked on the street in front of his house. He glanced at the license plate and noticed it was from Tennessee. Once the car came to a stop, Eddie and Vinh jumped from the vehicle and approached the van.

A large black man slid from the driver's side to the pavement. "Hey Henderson, about time you got home."

Eddie chuckled. "Damn, Carl, you got here earlier than I expected."

The two men embraced. Eddie looked Carl Johnston over, thinking he hadn't changed in the last ten years. Still tall, muscular, and soldierly. "You haven't changed a bit since the first time I saw you when we flew to Vietnam together." Eddie acted like he was going to hit him in the stomach. "Maybe put on a couple of pounds."

Carl laughed as he blocked the punch.

"Who's your friend?" Carl asked as he glanced at Vinh.

"You don't remember him?" Eddie smiled.

Carl walked toward Vinh and checked him out. "No, am I supposed to?"

"This is the boy, Vinh, who came to our unit after Mama-san got there." Eddie laughed. "He saved my life."

After Carl gave Vinh a bear hug, he lowered him to the ground. "Look at you, all grown up now. It's great to see you again."

Vinh's face flushed as he wiggled out of Carl's grasp. "You too."

Carl scanned the area around the road. "Where's Juan?"

"He's going to meet us at the hotel tomorrow." Eddie's eyes twinkled. "No sense him driving up here and then back down to Houston."

"Sounds good." Carl locked the van door. "How about a drink?"

Eddie sighed in satisfaction as he looked at the Carl and Vinh standing together. A smile spread across his face, showing his delight to be with his friends. He understood that they weren't perfect; neither was he. However, they had enough love in their hearts to show up at his time of need. They would defend him and his family without questioning what needed to be done. These were the friends that counted. He felt humbled and lucky to have Carl and Vinh in his life.

"I'm with you on that." Eddie took a step toward the house. "Let's go inside and I'll make us a drink."

The two men followed Eddie into the house and he led them to the kitchen. "Vinh, grab the Coke and some ice, please."

Carl pulled out a chair and took a seat, while Eddie got the glasses and bourbon.

Vinh filled each glass with ice and then poured Coke over the Jim Beam. He handed Carl a drink. Eddie and Vinh, each with a drink in hand, pulled out chairs and sat.

The room was quiet as each man sipped his bourbon.

Eddie broke the silence and raised his glass. "A toast to Ray, Bear, Cain, and Williams."

The three men clinked glasses.

"I want to thank you for coming when I needed you." Eddie shot a glance at Carl. "It means a lot."

Carl laughed. "That's what brothers do, man."

Before he realized it, the memories from his time with Juan and Carl in Vietnam appeared. The rescues and the firefights with the Viet Cong came alive in his thoughts. He heard the laughter and the banter that had filled their hooch. The friendship and brotherhood he felt for these men made him overcome with emotion.

"Tell us what you've been doing since you came home from 'Nam," Eddie said to Carl.

"Shit, it's been hard. I worked as a carpenter's apprentice for a couple of years. Work came and went, nothing steady. The truth is, I got fired. It took a while for me to learn to control my temper. For some reason, I was always angry."

"I know what you mean. I had the same problem." Eddie twirled the ice in his glass.

"Then I met an old friend of my father's," Carl continued. "He was going to retire as a private investigator, and he took me under his wing. Bob taught me everything I needed to know and helped me get my license. I've been doing this work ever since. Shit, I kinda like it." Carl sighed. "I have a lot of freedom."

"You ever get married? Have kids?" Eddie asked.

"No, not me. I like the ladies too much to pick just one." Carl laughed as he picked up his glass.

"I'll make everyone another drink." Vinh walked toward the sink.

"What about you, Vinh?" Carl asked.

There was silence until Vinh finished making the drinks.

Vinh pulled his chair out and sat. "There's not much to tell that you don't already know." He scanned the faces of the men at the table. "The Viet Cong took me from my village when I was eight. It was the Viet Cong that killed my mother. They taught me how to fight. I escaped right after Eddie did, and I hid in the jungle and then in my village. Then I met you at Chu Lai." Vinh smiled. "After the GIs left Vietnam, I got on a small boat to America. Many people died on the trip. First I lived in Houston and then Austin."

He stood and looked out the window.

"Fuck, think I'm going to quit my whining." Carl stood and put his arm around Vinh's shoulder, then he looked at Eddie with a twinkle in his eyes. "Okay, your turn."

"You guys know most of my story. Like you, I had anger issues. Hell, I couldn't drive down the road without calling everyone an asshole and giving them the finger. I even took my anger out on clerks and waitresses. I wasn't a nice guy." Eddie's lips tightened. "But I had Cheryl to help me through the bad times. I went on to get my degree and became a teacher. I like teaching. It was five years ago that I first ran into Dang at a restaurant in Berkeley." He hesitated, thinking of that moment. "I could've killed him then, but he disappeared."

Carl laughed. "A good thing you didn't kill him, or we wouldn't be together now."

"How about a toast?" Eddie held out his glass. "Welcome home."

They tapped glasses and said, "Welcome home."

Eddie stood with his shoulders squared. "I'll be right back."

He returned with a small box and set it on the table. Eddie removed papers and photographs, spreading them in the center of the table. "These are the drawings I made and photographs the detective took of the two buildings." Eddie surveyed the two men. "We need to come up with a plan to get Dang and Canh."

Vinh set a fresh drink in front of each of the men and then sat in his chair.

"How do you plan on doing it?" Carl asked.

"Well, that's what I said, Carl. I don't have a plan yet. That's what we need to generate. I hoped you might have some ideas, what with all your experience in the mix. So, shit, I've no real idea at this point." Eddie's forehead creased. "But I do believe it would be best to take them both out at the same time. So the warehouse seems the likely location—unless you have other ideas?"

Vinh pointed at the photographs of the warehouse. "Makes sense to me. When the three of us went to Little Saigon, that's where we saw them." He glanced at Eddie, then Carl. "Even when the detective went back to take pictures, that's where they seemed to hang out most of the time."

Eddie picked up the photo of the warehouse. "Okay, we'll plan on the warehouse being the primary location. Carl, that make sense to you?"

"Sure, sounds good." He nodded slowly.

"Well, we know he's normally surrounded by four or five men and drives a red Cadillac," Eddie said. "So those things help. Doesn't exactly keep a low profile. Arrogant bastard, in other words. Goes about the place like he's the fucking king. Entourage and all."

"Don't forget Dang's wife is with him most times, too," Vinh added.

"Do you know her?" Eddie asked.

"Yes, I do. Mrs. Dang was good to me. There were times that she gave me food and clothing. She even let me bathe at their house. She was kind." The corners of Vinh's mouth turned upward. "I'd like it if she didn't get hurt. I know that might be a tall order."

Eddie and Carl's faces contorted slightly. Finding times when the woman wasn't in their midst could be tricky. But Vinh was right—the fewer innocent people caught up in this shitstorm, the better.

Then Eddie grimaced again. How innocent could the woman be when she'd been married to that son of a bitch for so long? Surely she knew what Dang got up to, how he lived his life.

Difficult.

But he wasn't about to lay this on Vinh.

Eddie glanced at Vinh, looked him in the eyes. *Maybe . . .*

"That's good to know. You think she would help us?"

"She might." Vinh picked up a photograph of Mrs. Dang. "I'm not sure."

Vinh would have been young back when Mrs. Dang helped him, so there was more than a slight chance that she'd felt protective toward Vinh, knowing his situation. Maternal, even.

That could help them now, so long as she remembered him.

Carl pushed his chair back. "I'm getting some gear from the van."

Eddie slid the car keys to Vinh. "Would you go get us three pizzas? I think it's going to be a long night. So make 'em extra spicy to keep us awake." He laughed and handed Vinh money.

"You got it." Vinh headed for the door. "I'll be right back." He passed Carl as he stepped off the porch.

"Where are you going?" Carl asked.

"Getting pizzas," Vinh replied.

"Great, I'm starving. I want pineapple and ham on mine with extra cheese."

"You don't want spicy?" Vinh asked as he opened the car door.

"Nah, no spice for me. Gives me the shits."

"The boss said extra spice," Vinh protested.

"Well, now I'm the boss." Carl winked and then laughed.

Vinh smiled a broad smile. "Right, ham and cheese."

"And pineapple. Don't forget the pineapple."

Vinh rolled up his window and drove away.

Carl strolled back into the house and sauntered into the kitchen, carrying two small-sized canvas duffel bags. They looked worn and kind of dusty. He set the bags on the floor next to the table. Not only did they look ancient, but they were also heavy, judging by the fact Carl didn't even attempt to lift them onto a countertop.

Eddie lifted an eyebrow. "What's in the bags?"

Carl reached down and unzipped one of them.

"Can you close the curtains?"

Eddie moved around the table to the kitchen window and pulled the curtains closed. "Why are you acting so mysterious?"

When Carl stood, he held four pistols. "I thought we should each have a gun that isn't registered. These are completely off the system . . . anywhere in the world."

He set them down on the table near Eddie. "And here are four loaded magazines for each gun." Carl placed them next to the .45s.

"Damn, good thinking." Eddie picked up one of the pistols. "What else you got?"

He unzipped the second bag. "Didn't think you'd ever ask." Carl chuckled. "Here we have a stash of the best binoculars and radios. Each one of us will have a radio. You can see that they are small enough to carry in your pocket but heavy enough to bludgeon someone over the head and knock them out for a month of Sundays, if it comes to that."

Eddie laughed. "How in the hell did you get so smart?"

"I was born this way," Carl chuckled. "Anyway, that's not all." He set the binoculars and radios by the pistols. "I bought the van in

Tennessee and drove it here. The seller removed the vehicle identification number, and the license tag isn't registered. No one can trace it to us. That's a little bit too convenient, don't you think? Now what do you have to say, Eddie, pal? Am I clever enough to have earned us another bourbon or what?"

"Jesus, how did you learn to do all this stuff?"

"In my business, you have to learn a lot of shortcuts." Carl glanced at Eddie. "And you meet a lot of unsavory people to teach you what you don't know. Close protection courses are one thing—they're full of protocol says this, and the law says that. In the real world, we often have to make up the rules as we go along."

Eddie nodded that he understood and urged him to continue. The two examined the gear, pulling out one piece at a time.

"Coming in with pizza!" Vinh yelled.

The front door slammed shut, and Vinh strolled into the kitchen, his arms laden with large flat boxes. The smell was delicious. "Hey, guys, you want to clean the table off? Looks like you got a pile of good stuff there, but my stomach's growling already."

The two men removed the weapons, ammo, and other equipment and stowed it all back in the duffel bags. Eddie collected the photographs and other material strewed across the table.

"Thanks." Vinh slid the pizzas onto the counter.

Eddie grabbed plates and flatware. "Here you go. We can eat civilized." He made everyone another Jim Beam and Coke.

The kitchen was quiet as the men wolfed down slice after slice of pizza. It appeared to Eddie that each man was deep in his own thoughts. He assumed they were thinking about what would happen once they got to Little Saigon.

Enjoying the silence, Eddie leaned back in his chair, letting the moment soak into his bones. He closed his eyes for a second, recalling the last time he'd been with the men sitting around the table—it was in Vietnam. For the first time in months, his body relaxed. He felt safe now that his brothers were with him.

He noticed that each of their faces was expressionless even though they knew what they were about to do. At that moment,

Eddie realized the sacrifice they would make for him. He questioned if he would do the same. Could he leave Cheryl and the boys and go to another state and kill someone to complete a favor for another guy?

There was no way he could ever repay his brothers.

He hoped when this was over that he wouldn't have new nightmares—and that they wouldn't either.

Carl let out a loud belch and pushed away the empty plate. "Okay, what's the plan, boys?"

Vinh cleared the table of the pizza boxes, plates, and flatware. Eddie slid the pictures of the warehouse and union building onto the table again.

Carl reached across, organizing the photographs by location, jabbing a hefty finger into each one as he set it down like he knew there wasn't a plan.

"Right. Pay attention and listen up." Carl gazed at the two men. "Here's how things will go down." It was as though his brain must run on pizza and bourbon. Now he was at full strength. "We'll work in teams. Vinh and Eddie, you'll work together. And Juan and I are a team." He looked back at Eddie. "I'm looking at you as second in command. Please confirm your understanding."

Eddie's eyebrows rose for a second, as if questioning how Carl had demoted him on his own fucking job. Then he smiled. "Roger that."

"Where's our base going to be, Eddie?" Carl asked. "Hopefully, a hotel that is cheapish, but comfortable. And no place filled with lowlifes. Don't want to do a good job of this only to get caught up in someone else's screw-up. You know, cops show up to a drunken brawl, everyone gets searched, shit like that. Way I see it, every detail needs to be perfect. I ain't doing this shit twice."

Eddie glanced around the table, nodding. Carl made a lot of sense. Luckily, he was ready with an answer for the boss.

"We'll stay at a motel off the interstate. Juan has the address. It's only a couple of miles from Little Saigon. Clean little place, quiet. We could be the only guests if we're lucky. And we should be able to get this done and be back here in a couple of days. Unless Dang never shows, of course."

"Hmm, couple of days, maybe. I'd say it should be more like three," Carl shifted in his chair. "You want to arrive leisurely, afternoon if possible, hang out a few hours in the room, shower, have a doze, make it look as if you're there for a break, not straight-in-straight-out on some kind of business, you know? Because what often gives these operations away is that guys are too nervous. They show up to the motel jittery, shifty-eyed and waiting to check out before they even pick up their room keys, hiding their trucks around the back, only moving about after dark, that kind of nonsense. We don't do any of that. We're four fellas on a nostalgia trip down memory lane, with all the time in the world. You with me so far?"

"Sure, we're with you." Eddie picked up a picture of the warehouse.

Vinh looked impressed and nodded.

It was shaping up to be a good plan already.

"If you don't mind me asking," Vinh asked, slightly deferentially as if scared the big man might kick him off the team for being a slow learner, "what's day three going to be for? I take it day one's a recon sometime after we arrive, same day . . . and then day two's a recon plus action? Sorry to ask."

Carl tapped his heavy metal pen like an impatient drummer. "Sure, sure. Ask away. Better ask now than leave it to when you're lying dead in a gutter because you didn't ask."

They laughed, but this was serious stuff.

"Day three is to wind down, if you see what I mean. After we do the job, we do the opposite of what assholes who commit murder do. We don't get the hell outta town that same night. We look around, get seen in town in daylight, enjoy the scenery. Hang on that bit longer to not be that car everyone sees speeding away. And three days is like an extended honeymoon." He laughed loudly at his joke.

"Fuck me, man." Eddie chuckled. "I'm not marrying you! No matter how much you fucking pay me!"

They all hooted with laughter. More drinks got poured, more ice, then more serious faces, leaning in, looking at every small detail of all the images spread on the table before them. Carl resumed tapping his pen and then pointed at the picture of the warehouse.

"Juan and I can keep watch on the warehouse. You and Vinh observe the union building. Whichever one Dang goes to, that team radios the other. They're only a couple of minutes apart. And we don't move from our positions, right? Not for anything."

"Right," Eddie said.

"What if we need a break?" Vinh asked in all earnestness. "I mean, it can get chilly standing in one spot . . ."

Carl's face showed that he was not amused. "I say it again, nobody moves!" He seemed irritated now, intent on this job getting done right.

It was no longer old pals having a laugh. Carl drew a hard line.

"Okay. That will work." Eddie rubbed at his jaw. "The hardest part will be separating Dang and Canh from the other men with them. And from Mrs. Dang, if she's there on the day. We only want those two. No one else needs to get hurt."

He looked each man in the eye and waited for him to nod that he understood, or to comment that he disagreed. "That's going to be the hardest part of this mission."

"So, the kill is the easy part, you reckon?" Carl's eyebrows were somewhere heading for the back of his head. His face again had that *you gotta be kidding, talking shit like this* look.

"Well, no. I mean, point taken." He squirmed now. Eddie had rarely played second fiddle to anyone in his life before—well, only to Cheryl now and again—and this second-in-charge thing was hitting him harder than he hoped his expression was demonstrating. He felt like a rookie.

"I did get your point, Eddie." Carl's eyes flashed. "As in war, we protect the innocent as best we can. But we also must tolerate that those who are not the exact target but who are in on it—such as the wife—may fall as casualties anyway, despite our best efforts. You with me? All agreed?"

"Yep," both men said. Vinh's face was ashen, and Eddie assumed he was thinking of the kindly Missus Dang being killed or maimed by accident. Vinh's eyes watered and he brushed at his nose with a sleeve.

"So, we are on to the hardest part. How are we going to kill them?" Carl asked. "What are your ideas, Eddie?"

While Eddie digested Carl's words, there was silence at the table. Tonight was the first time he had heard someone outside the family say those words. "Kill them" brought a whole new vibe to what they discussed.

Carl was never one for euphemisms. He would always go right in and say what needed saying. When the enemy killed guys back in 'Nam, some of their team would say, *he went to a better place, met his maker,* or *gone to join his old ma in heaven.*

Not Carl.

"Poor fucker. We'll never find his head," or even once or twice, "He'll never have to worry about finding that one missing sock again." Those were the kinds of things Carl said, too matter-of-factly for most.

But everyone knew it wasn't mean. Simply direct. There was no messing with words around Carl.

"C'mon, fellas. How we gonna kill these bastards?"

Eddie looked at his friends, his brothers, with their jaws set and shoulders squared. They were in killing mode. There'd be no turning back.

Eddie forced a smile. "Play that by ear," he said, expecting another rocket up his ass from the boss. But this time, none came.

Carl tap-tapped his pen again, his lips crooked as he was deep in thought. "Right," Carl finally said. "As much as it shames me to admit it, we have no way to plan beyond this point, since we have no idea what's inside the buildings or who will be with him."

There was no way to scope out the interior of the warehouse without drawing attention to themselves. It was what it was.

Carl glanced around the room at his silent team members.

"One thing's certain, we need to execute them. A, that's how they deserve to die. And B, it will make the right impression when the police show up. Get them to believe it's gang-related. Cops have markedly less time for shit that goes down between gangs."

Without a word, the other two men nodded their agreement.

After Eddie stood, he stacked the photos into a pile and placed them in the box. "Let's get some sleep. Carl, you can sleep in the boys' room."

"What time we leaving?" Carl asked.

Eddie looked at his watch. "I figured we would leave around zero-six-thirty and stop along the way for breakfast." He picked up the box. "Is that okay with you guys?"

"That's good with me." Carl stood.

"Go ahead, and I'll clean up the kitchen." Eddie pushed his chair to the table.

Once Vinh and Carl were asleep, Eddie glanced at the photographs one last time as he sat on his bed. The more anxious he became, the more the realization of what he was about to do tugged at his sense of right and wrong. However, his festering guilt of how Dang had hurt Cheryl and murdered Ray made thoughts of killing him easier.

There was no right time or right motive to execute a man, no matter what. But if there was, this would meet all the criteria.

Eddie pulled the sheets over himself, switching out his bedside lamp.

His conscience was as clear as it had ever been.

CHAPTER 19

A PLAN TO EXECUTE

After he woke, Vinh went to each room, shaking his friends awake from a deep sleep.

In silence, everyone organized their personal belongings for the trip to Houston. Carl was the first to the van, opening a rear door and arranging his backpack and the two duffel bags into the cargo area.

Carl had spent the last hour at the kitchen table, all the weapons and equipment laid out in front of him. He tested each item methodically and meticulously, making sure each piece of gear earned its place.

Even the way Carl laid out the items in the cargo area was with care. He knew what went precisely where, and then inside each canvas bag, he knew the order of all the gear, right down to the last spare battery and the sizes of the four pairs of stowed black gloves.

Eddie and Vinh followed him outside, placing their packs alongside Carl's. Eddie slammed the rear door shut.

"I got something for you guys, back in the house. Hope everything fits." Carl's expression was serious. "Let's head back inside for two minutes."

It was still dark and there was no one about, but donning and doffing the gear out in the open posed a risk of being spotted. Carl would never make that kind of thoughtless error.

In the hallway, he grabbed the one duffel bag he'd earlier kicked under the tall coat stand; this one looked soft and over-stuffed. He pulled at the lashing on the neck to reveal a mass of black outerwear.

The men reached in and pulled out a black zip-up sweater and a baseball hat each. Carl had taken the gear from his workplace. There was a rectangular cut-out where the security company logo used to be on the collar and breast of each item, and the front of the cap.

"Now, Eddie, you got a clothes iron or a press, something like that?"

It was an odd question.

"Um, I think Cheryl has an iron."

He knew not to ask stupid questions now, especially not of Carl, though his mind said *what the fuck?*

Carl had believed the sweaters would help conceal their pistols, and the pockets were about large enough to carry the radios.

The caps might help hide their faces.

But with large chunks missing on each breast and the caps, it would look strange and draw more attention. So he'd come up with a bright idea.

A pal of his worked at Burger King and had managed to get some embroidered iron-on patches with the BK logo, and Carl had collected them on his way to Eddie's place. Now they had a cover story of being four Burger King area managers on an "away day" to see how other area operations worked.

Many men who attempted to be undercover were too damn obvious; their military-style dress often gave it away, or they chose something that stood out. All these four needed to do was stink like burger grease and they had their cover for as long as they liked. They wore their new gear with jeans and sneakers.

"Good idea, boss!" Eddie enthused. "But there's a downside."

"And that is?"

"Well, I was hoping to stop by a Burger King later. I usually treat myself after a tough day. And this is sure to fall into that category."

Everyone laughed.

New logos in place, they passed the garments around, trying things on until everyone got the right sizes. The gloves would only come out later when the firearms were about to be distributed and prepped on site.

"I figured the hat and sweater might identify us as a friendly if things got hectic." Carl smiled.

"Cool. Kinda like having a uniform. It also means we can talk about food when people ask. Good idea." Eddie zipped his sweater and adjusted his hat.

"Pal." Carl shot a disapproving look. "Your cap isn't right."

He looked at himself in the mirror.

"Not a millimeter out of place!" Eddie protested.

"Exactly my point." Carl chuckled. "You're supposed to be a burger flipper, remember? Not elite forces."

"Ah." Eddie tweaked it. He was feeling stupid again. These were silly errors that could cost lives, draw attention. Eddie glanced at his friends. "Okay, let's do this."

He clambered into the front passenger side as Carl climbed behind the wheel. Vinh scrambled through the side door, sitting on the floor behind the driver seat.

Carl rotated the key in the ignition, and the eight cylinders roared to life. The sound of the engine echoed throughout the van. Carl accelerated as he wheeled the vehicle into the street, driving to I-35.

On the interstate, the loud hum of the engine discouraged conversation.

Roughly thirty minutes on the highway, the van braked hard, and Carl's two bags slid next to Vinh. "Sorry about that, guys. Looks like an accident down the road. Fucking long line of traffic."

Vinh looked between the two seats to see out the front window. "Damn, how much longer until we eat? I'm starving."

"There's a Denny's not far from here." Eddie ruffled Vinh's hair. "Hang on—we'll get you some food."

Needing a distraction, Vinh opened the bag with the radios. He pulled two out and passed one to Eddie.

"I'm Victor, and you're Echo. Those are our call signs."

He turned on the radio.

After a moment, Eddie figured out how to turn on his radio. He spoke into the microphone, "Victor, this is Echo, over."

Vinh smiled. "Echo, this is Victor, go ahead, over."

Carl turned in his seat. "What are you two up to?"

"Practicing radio procedures." Vinh laughed. "You're Charlie, and Juan is Juliet."

He smiled. "Roger that." Carl turned back to face the front, shaking his head.

The traffic began to move, slowly at first, and then the van started to pick up speed as it rolled along the highway. Within forty minutes, Carl turned off the interstate, pulling into Denny's parking lot. It was full; kids shouted and screamed in cars, and harried moms rolled strollers along the pavement.

Vinh's head popped up.

"Alright, show me the food! My gut's about to eat itself!"

The two in the front turned and stared. *Jesus.*

This kid was always hungry, and God only knew where he put all that food he went through. He was as lean as a rake.

"Still growing or something?" Carl asked. "Maybe you got worms."

Vinh laughed, but it was evident that the boy's constant talk of eating was bothering Carl. "Let me tell you something before you stuff yourself so full of carbs and fizzy soda that you can't think straight," Carl ventured, addressing Vinh. "When I'm at work, we go days without food. And I do mean days. We're holed up in a van someplace, on surveillance, heads down, keepin' low. You know? Can't leave for a pizza, ya know? Life's tough in the real world, Vinh. On my shifts, you won't eat, won't sleep, won't talk, won't take a piss. And depending on how this next job goes for us, maybe you two will be getting to see the real world sooner than you hope."

Eddie was pissed at the *you two* part, but he said nothing.

Of all people, he was sure he'd already seen more than enough of the real world with all that he'd been through back in 'Nam, and with Dang since. He felt he'd seen it all ten thousand times.

Carl was great, and certainly he knew his stuff when it came to security details, but he sure could be a pain in the ass sometimes. He talked about the job as if no other man on earth could do it.

The truth was that any ex-military guy could walk into private security.

Okay, maybe not own his own company and do that well, but they would have a chance to kick some ass.

"Fuck you, man," Eddie said quietly, almost under his breath.

"Heard that." Carl rolled his eyes. "Supersonic ears. Goes with the job too."

They all laughed as they jumped from the van onto the pavement.

"I hear you, boss." Eddie chuckled. Nothing could dampen their camaraderie much; it had been way too long in the making.

Vinh slid the side door open and scrambled outside.

The men strolled into the restaurant like a posse of cowboys from out of town. Once the food was delivered, the three of them ate in silence.

Carl watched Vinh, ensuring the young man didn't stuff too many carbs down his gullet or eat too fast.

Eddie glanced from one to the other and back again, the magnitude of their undertaking hitting home once more.

How can I ever repay that debt of friendship?

The waitress brought three coffees to go. Eddie paid the cashier for the meals and they went back to the van. Everyone climbed into the same position in the vehicle they had occupied earlier.

Eddie turned in his seat. "Next stop, the motel in Houston."

The men laughed as Carl turned the ignition and the van's engine roared. He wheeled onto the interstate on-ramp, gathering speed as he entered the highway.

The remainder of the trip didn't take long, though the pace and occasional bumps made Vinh holler from the back, "Slow down. I'm trying to drink my coffee!"

Carl turned off the highway and drove into the motel parking lot. He found a vacant spot near the front entrance, then reached for his drink, now only lukewarm with a frothy top.

With the van parked and all three occupants still drinking their coffees, a short Hispanic man jumped out of a red Mazda and strode toward the group, a broad beaming grin across his face.

"Look, here comes Juan." Eddie pointed in the man's direction.

"Well! Look who it is. Mi amigo!" Carl cried, replacing his drink in the holder and flinging the car door open wide.

Carl was already out of the car, and Juan jumped into his arms as if they were long-lost brothers.

"Man, you haven't changed a bit." Juan eyed Carl top to toe.

"And you're as little as ever," Carl quipped, then put Juan back on the ground. "It's great to see you again, buddy."

Carl looked around at his friends. "It's great to see all of you, in case I didn't make that clear earlier. Even if you do need whipping into shape."

He winked and clapped Juan's back again with a hefty palm. Then he looked around for cameras on the outside of the motel. He turned to Juan. "Buddy, before we go in, you gotta put on your uniform. We're a team, starting right now."

"Huh? My . . . my what? Uniform?" He looked puzzled.

Carl flung open the cargo hold of the van and pulled out the now-sagging duffel bag. "Here. Cap and sweater. Congratulations on your promotion to Burger King area manager. It was tough to get hold of a manager's sweater in a kiddie size." He laughed at his joke.

"No shit!" Juan chuckled. "Always wanted a job at Burger King. What kind of salary does this come with?"

Carl tapped Juan on the back of the head. "A fat kick up the ass. Now get a move on."

Eddie opened the back door and motioned to Vinh, who was standing around looking like a spare part. He always seemed to feel a little awkward when the older men messed around and joked.

"Let's grab our bags." Eddie turned back to address them all. "I'll go get us two rooms. Vinh and I will share one, and you guys can share the other. You okay with that?"

"Sure, it isn't a problem for me." Carl smiled. "Me and Juan in one room, you and Vinh in the other. Makes sense."

Juan looked confused, but shrugged. "All good for me, too. Whichever room I'm in, cool."

"Great." Eddie looked at Vinh. "Can you grab my bag?"

"You got it." Vinh reached into the van to grab the luggage.

They gathered in the small lobby while Eddie checked in and left a deposit. He'd decided to use an assumed name when registering.

Once he received the keys, he approached his friends. "Here's your key. The rooms are next to each other with an adjoining door that could be handy. I suggest we make full use of it."

"Why? You gonna miss me that much?" Carl's eyes twinkled. "You need to tuck me in at night?"

"Cut the crap," Eddie replied. "You know what I mean. Less hallway time, less chance of being seen in and out too much. Good for late-night briefings around our drinks."

Everyone nodded and smiled.

"So, let's put our shit away, take a few hours so we don't look like we came here with a job to do, and then head over to Little Saigon," Eddie said. "Well, there'll also be a shower for me. Don't want to look too much like I wore this sweatshirt for a week, unlike the real burger guys."

Without a word, the four men walked up the stairs and along the hallway, each looking forward to a nice hot shower and a short nap before heading off later for the first recon.

Once inside, the first thing Carl did was open the door between the two rooms. Eddie threw his bag on the bed and then closed the curtains.

Carl peeked into Eddie's room. "Hey guys, come over here."

When Eddie and Vinh walked in, Carl was placing one of the bags on the small desk.

"Might as well distribute the equipment right now so we're all set."

He unzipped the bag. "Here you go." Carl handed each of the others a pistol with two magazines. Juan and Vinh inspected their weapon to make sure it was clear of ammo.

Eddie looked for a magazine and then slid the barrel back, checking the chamber. Next, he released the barrel, letting it slide forward, and then inserted a magazine. Once situated, Eddie slid the pistol into his waistband, allowing the oversized T-shirt to conceal it.

"Good drills." Carl said, but he looked surprised at the same time. "Do you honestly think I didn't check all that shit before we even set off?"

But it was good to see "the team" doing what they'd long ago learned.

Before they finished checking the pistols, Carl had unzipped the second bag and handed out the radios. "I have extra batteries if you need some. There's an indicator on the top right side." He pointed to the location. "It's best to check it often. Battery life isn't the greatest. And I don't want any of that, oh, but my battery ran out shit. That's all I got, so you'll each take care of it, right?"

"Right," came a trio of voices.

Stick your spares right up where the sun don't shine. Eddie laughed to himself as a broad smile traversed his face. "What's the radio range?" Eddie asked, hoping it was an intelligent question as far as the boss was concerned. But Carl's eyes narrowed anyway.

"About a half-mile? Maybe a little more, if we're lucky. Should be good enough for how we're using them. It's only if we get separated that we'd have to be careful."

Separated?

Not a pleasant thought for anyone.

They all knew what that meant.

If the job gets fucked up.

•

They were rested and set. Carl squared his shoulders.

"Okay, let's go." He glanced around the room. "Juan, make sure to bring the two duffel bags. We don't want any equipment left in the room. No telling who might see it."

"Good point." Juan and Vinh picked up the two bags.

The men exited Carl's room, taking long strides toward the van. They carried themselves like men on a mission—shoulders back, standing tall, walking in step with each other.

Not a smile or a joke between them now.

But whenever they encountered anyone, they fell into cover mode, joking and jostling each other like the Burger King managers whose regular lives they must appear to assume.

Once at the van, Juan opened the side door for Vinh and both men climbed into the back. Carl reached around Juan and threw the bags into the rear cargo area. He slammed the door shut and scrambled into the driver seat. Momentarily, he looked at Eddie and turned the ignition key.

As the van rumbled down the frontage road, Eddie thought the next couple of hours might pass quickly—or it could be the final battle that he would ever fight. At times, the memory of Dang ordering Canh to hit Cheryl surfaced, and it was hard to keep his mind focused.

He knew that his three friends watched him, expecting him to show strength, to keep his fears and grief at bay. And because of his inevitable weaknesses and emotions, especially over the loss of baby Ray, they no longer thought of him as their leader for this job—but he still commanded their full respect.

Carl turned the van down Bellaire Boulevard.

He slowed, noticing the heavy traffic that flowed in both directions.

"Let's park under the tree where we did last time." Eddie pointed to the parking lot to his right.

When he neared the entrance, Carl turned on the turn signal. "I see it. It appears to be empty, too." He coasted to a stop under the tree. "This should give us some concealment. Couldn't be better."

Eddie shifted in his seat. He mentally reviewed the plan to find and isolate Dang and Canh. What had appeared a good idea last night now seemed filled with flaws. As he looked around the street, he saw how inadequate his knowledge was—both of the area and the people he sought.

Eddie had to find the spark that brought back his confidence. He glanced at Carl, then Juan and then at Vinh, recalling why they had so quickly joined with him. Yes, they were brothers, but they too wanted revenge against Dang. He had caused them all pain.

"Remember not to do anything on your own. This is a team effort. Keep a check on your emotions at all times. If you're going to take any kind of action, call the other team first. Got it?" Carl glanced at each of the men. "We need to act together to do what we need to do."

The three men nodded in affirmation.

Without hesitation, Eddie threw the van door open, letting the crisp winter air into the vehicle. "Okay, let's go to our positions and find these sons of bitches."

For once, Carl didn't need to say anything.

GOSSIP IS THE TRUTH

With hands in pockets, Carl and Juan strolled along the sidewalk toward the restaurant to keep watch on the warehouse, while Eddie and Vinh crossed the busy street heading toward the union headquarters building. They did their best to blend into the background and act like tourists.

Eddie and Vinh strode another block west of the warehouse, pushing past the hundreds of pedestrians moving along the sidewalk like an army of ants. As they got closer, Eddie spotted a small restaurant where they could sit and watch the office.

Once inside, they sat at a table with a clear line of sight of the union building. There were Vietnamese customers at the other tables, talking and laughing as they enjoyed a late Saturday morning meal. They barely looked up when the two unfamiliar men entered.

As Eddie looked around, he noticed that most were eating a particular type of sandwich. "What's that they're eating?"

"It's called a *bánh mì*, a Vietnamese breakfast sandwich." Vinh glanced at the man and woman at the table next to theirs. "It's a baguette loaded with pickled daikon and carrot, cilantro, spicy chilies, and a sliver of cucumber stuffed with sweet minced pork."

Eddie's nose wrinkled. "Do you think I'll like it?"

Vinh smiled. "Yes, I do. It's hearty and tasty."

"Okay, you talked me into it." Eddie raised his hand to signal the waitress.

An attractive young Vietnamese woman wearing blue jeans and a red sweater came to the table. "What can I get for you two?"

"We'll have two of the banh mi sandwiches and two Cokes, please." Eddie flashed his boyish grin. "I hope I pronounced the sandwich correctly."

"Not bad. Well, for a Texan anyway."

The waitress giggled and went toward the kitchen.

The two men sat in silence while they stared at the union headquarters. They checked out pedestrians as they neared the building or passed by, hoping to recognize a member of Dang's group.

Eddie's body tingled with excitement.

Without him knowing, a smirk tugged at the corner of his lips as he stared at the building. He imagined that Dang would appear at any minute now, and he could exact the revenge he deserved.

While waiting for his food, Eddie looked around the room to see if any patron seemed to have a particular interest in Vinh and him.

The customers appeared to be busy eating or conversing rather than paying any attention to him. Evidently, the banh mi was all-engrossing.

The waitress approached the table balancing two plates in one hand and two Cokes in another. "Two *bánh mì* and two Cokes." She slid the order onto the table. "If you need anything else, please let me know."

Eddie smiled. "We'll do that."

He picked up his sandwich and took a bite.

"What do you think?" Vinh poked at the ice in his glass of Coke.

"Damn, you're right. It's spicy, salty, savory, and sweet all rolled into one great flavor. Love it." Eddie grinned. "Thanks for talking me into ordering it."

As Vinh took a large bite of his sandwich, he pointed at the union building. "Look, it's the Cadillac." He swallowed the bite whole, washing it down with the drink. "Looks like a woman driving."

The car door opened and a middle-aged Vietnamese woman stepped out. She wore a tight-fitting black skirt to show off her small waist, and also heels and a white blouse.

"It's Dang's wife."

"Fuck." Eddie sat straight in his chair. "I mean, it's good because we know they're there. But she's the one you don't want hurt."

Vinh turned and stared at Eddie. "No, we all don't want her hurt."

"Right . . . Right."

Eddie was glad not to be in charge right now, because saying stuff was one thing. Adhering to it, when he knew there could be a chance to nail his enemy, was another. What kind of a woman would stay married to Dang?

But he was suddenly distracted by more activity.

The door to the union office opened and a big Vietnamese man walked out to greet Mrs. Dang. He stopped and gave a small bow to the woman. The way her arms flailed around, it seemed she was upset with him.

Vinh leaned forward in his seat. "That's the man I shot at your house and kicked in the face the last time we were here."

Eddie's brows drew together. "You sure? So, he's the one that held Cheryl when Canh hit her?"

He drained his drink and set the glass on the table.

"I'm positive." Vinh's gaze turned back to the man.

"What are you two staring at?" the waitress said.

Eddie jumped and turned to face her. When he did, his elbow knocked over his glass, sending ice skittering across the table. "What the heck?" He was caught off guard and upset.

The woman started to mop up the ice. "I'm sorry I startled you." She picked up his glass. "You two were so engrossed watching something. I wanted to head on over and join in the fun. I'm sorry."

"That's okay." Eddie picked up ice cubes. "I'm the one that should apologize. It's just, I'm a bit deaf and when someone creeps up and . . . well, you know. But do you know that woman by the red car?"

She gazed out the window. "Oh, sure! That's Mrs. Dang. She's the wife of the union boss." She looked down at Eddie. "I know her fairly well. We talk at the union meetings. My husband is a shrimper and he hates Mr. Dang." She nervously surveyed the dining area. "She's not happy in her marriage. Mr. Dang is cruel and won't let her leave him. The man you see her talking to is with her most of the time. The rumor is, Mr. Dang has him watch her. Pays him to do it."

"Wow, how do you know that for sure?" Vinh asked.

The waitress turned her gaze to Vinh, rolling her eyes. "Because she told me so." Before she turned to leave, she glanced at Eddie. "Do you need another Coke?"

Eddie leaned back in his chair. "Yes, two, please." He turned his attention back to Mrs. Dang.

At that moment, she stormed into the building. The man looked around the area and then stepped inside, closing the door behind him.

As he watched, Eddie said to Vinh, "I need to get in there and talk to her."

"Why? What can she do for us?" Vinh had a quizzical look on his face.

"If she really hates her husband that much, maybe she'll help us." Eddie put his elbows on the table and leaned in toward Vinh. "Hell, she might set it up, the where and when—for us to get Dang!"

He was animated, his cheeks all pink and rosy, his eyes flashing.

This was the best news ever! Well, for a long time, anyhow.

"Eddie, what if the waitress is full of shit," Vinh whispered. "What if it's gossip?"

"Well, I watched her face, body, and eyes. I believe she's telling the truth." Eddie's eyes widened.

"That's putting a lot of trust in intuition." Vinh's lips turned downward. "Is it worth getting killed if what she said isn't true?"

"Vinh, I'm going to follow my gut on this one." Eddie winked.

The waitress returned, setting the Cokes in front of the two men. "Anything else?"

"Just the check, please." Eddie reached for his wallet.

She pulled it out of her apron, handing it to Eddie. "There you go."

"Thanks." He read the check, pulled out cash, and laid it on the table.

The waitress picked up the money and strolled to another customer.

Eddie turned his attention back to the union office. Within seconds, the heavyset man opened the door and strode toward the car. He crawled into the driver's seat. "The guard is leaving."

Eddie stood, excitement coursing through his body.

"You don't have to do this," Vinh said as he stood.

Deep down in his gut Eddie had a feeling that told him, *don't do it*, but all his instincts told him, *do it*. He understood that by finding courage instead of succumbing to the fear, he would get Dang. Talking with Dang's wife might be the best way to get him.

"Yes, I do. Come on, let's go outside." Eddie had a twisted smile plastered on his face.

The car backed onto the road, and then the driver squealed the tires as he headed west.

Vinh and Eddie left the restaurant, taking long strides along the sidewalk toward the building. Eddie stopped at an alley right before crossing the main road and pulled out the radio.

"Charlie, this is Echo," Eddie transmitted.

"Go ahead Echo," Carl replied.

"I'm going in to talk to Dang's wife. She's alone. I think she might help us."

"Man, are you sure?" Carl asked. His tone didn't say *are you sure?* It said, *fuck man, you're some crazy motherfucker*. "That's not the plan. What we do, we do together."

Eddie looked up and down the sidewalk. "I'm doing it. I know it's good. I'll leave Vinh out front, but I want you guys to come here now and wait with him." He gazed down the alley. "If I get into any trouble, I'll push the talk button two times and the three of you can come on in to help." He licked his lips. "If someone approaches the building, push the talk button twice, and I'll get out of there. Got it?"

Eddie's emotions were now in control—and those emotions might determine whether they all lived or died.

Carl's face was darker now, all the veins in his head about to burst. "Yep, we're on the way. You be careful and don't do anything fucking stupid."

"Roger that. Talk later." Eddie eased the radio back into his sweater pocket.

He stared into Vinh's eyes. "When we cross the street, go sit by that tree at the end of the driveway and be a lookout for me. The guys will be here in a couple of minutes." He put his hand on Vinh's shoulder. "You need to stay put. If everything goes okay, I'll get you when I leave." Eddie squeezed his shoulder. "You understand?"

"Yes, but it's not smart to go in alone. Like Carl said . . ." Vinh's eyes narrowed. He came to an abrupt halt in his speech, knowing when to shut up. "But I'll be here for you."

The two men jogged across the street. Vinh stopped right by the tree, giving Eddie a wave as he continued to the office.

Once at the main door, Eddie slowly turned the handle, pulling the door toward him. When it was halfway open, he slid himself through. He paused to let his eyes adjust to the poorly lit room, gazing around at the cluttered desks and old metal filing cabinets. The room had a musty odor and a strong smell of Vietnamese food.

A voice called out, "Who's that?"

Eddie's eyes darted around the room. "Mrs. Dang?"

A shadow appeared from a narrow hallway. "Can I help you?"

"Yes, ma'am, my name's Eddie. I need to talk to you about your husband." He removed his hat, which allowed his hair to fall free.

She strode to the middle of the room only a couple of feet from Eddie. "What about my husband?"

Eddie observed her clear, wrinkle-free face, her dark almond eyes with her long black hair resting on her shoulders. Her full lips were set tight. She looked like a Vietnamese princess.

"I need to find him. He needs to pay for what he did to others over the years." His eyes gleamed with hatred.

"I don't know what you mean." Mrs. Dang stood straighter. "My driver will be back any minute. You should leave."

Eddie took a step toward her. "Please hear me out. It's important."

She hesitated while staring into his eyes.

"Go ahead. But you only have a couple of minutes."

"I knew him in the war. He executed my friend after he tortured us. I witnessed him killing villagers and stealing their belongings. He even took their children and taught them to kill." Eddie's face turned red from the pent-up anger he released on her. "A couple of months ago, he tried to blow up my car, but he blew up the wrong one and almost killed a young girl."

"Look, there is nothing you can say that will shock or surprise me." Her eyes closed. "I know he is a bad man."

She sighed, crumpling into an office chair, looking as if she had heard it all before. Eddie didn't doubt many had come to her before him. He was probably the latest in a long and unending line.

Eddie sat next to her. "After that, your husband and three other men broke into my home. He ordered Canh to hit my pregnant wife in the stomach, killing our son."

"Oh, I'm so sorry." Her face fell, and she sobbed, placing her hand on Eddie's.

For a moment, he regretted telling her about her husband, but he couldn't stop now. He needed to tell her everything to win her over. He couldn't think about sparing her the pain of having to hear his words.

"There's more to tell." He squeezed her hand. "I am sorry."

She pulled her hand away.

"What more can there be?"

She stood and backed away from Eddie.

He felt his radio vibrate two times.

Shit, someone's coming.

•

Vinh stood and nodded toward the street. "Look, it's the Cadillac."

"I signaled Eddie." Carl slid the radio back into his pocket. "Vinh, walk away so he doesn't recognize you."

Without a word, he turned and walked along the sidewalk in the opposite direction of the car.

Juan stood and took a drink from a flask. "I got this." He staggered into the middle of the road, acting as if he was heaving.

The heavyset man stopped the car, now blocking the traffic, and rolled down the window. "Get out of my way, you drunken Mexican."

"I'm not Mexican . . . I'm Hispanic." Juan staggered to the car, staring at the driver with wild eyes. "So what are you? Look like a fat gook to me." He made sure the smell of alcohol followed his words.

The driver's eyes narrowed as he opened the car door.

Out of nowhere, Carl appeared with his cap pulled low over his eyes.

"I'm sorry, sir. I'll get this drunken asshole out of your way."

"Thank you." The man climbed back behind the wheel of the car.

•

Eddie's eyes narrowed. "I have to go. But you need to know that your husband killed your son." He stepped toward the side door.

"No, that can't be, Bao wouldn't kill Đức." Tears ran down her cheeks. "How do you know this?"

He turned to face her. "My friend Vinh was there and witnessed him killing—no, executing—your son."

"Vinh saw this? But he was only a boy, too. Are you sure?" She cried. "Bao is a cruel man, but he wouldn't. Not this."

"He executed him. There's no doubt." Eddie touched her hand. "Your son was a kind person."

"He was a baby, my baby." She took a step toward Eddie. "Where are you staying?"

"We're at the Motel Royal, room 206, off the frontage road. Come at eight this evening." Eddie stepped through the side doorway.

"I'll be there," she muttered.

As he closed the door, he heard a man's voice, "Mrs. Dang, I'm back from my meeting." Eddie pushed through a row of bushes and walked along the drive adjacent to the office until he reached the street.

"Man, that was close." Carl gave Eddie a brief hug. "We need to talk when we get back to the hotel."

"I don't know how you did it, but it took him a while to get to the building after you signaled me." Eddie stepped from Carl's grasp.

Carl laughed, pointing at Juan. "Hell, that crazy Mexican blocked the son of a bitch's car! Acting like he was drunk! That's enough distraction for anyone. Even the gook."

"Thanks, pal." Eddie punched Juan in the arm. "I owe you a big one!"

With a smile, Juan held out his flask. "Want a drink?"

"No thanks." Eddie chuckled, pushing his hand away. Maybe Juan's little ploy hadn't been so much of an act. He stank like a distillery. The guy drank enough booze to kill a man—and he did it daily.

"What now?" Vinh asked.

Eddie's lips curved into a smile. "Let's go back to the hotel and I'll tell you all about my conversation with Mrs. Dang."

Once Carl pulled onto the main road, he turned on the radio. The radio blared, "We Gotta Get Out of This Place" by The Animals. Everyone sat silently.

CHAPTER 21

MEETING A WOMAN

The brakes squealed and the van shuddered to a stop, waking the men from their short nap. "We're here." Carl opened the driver's door and slid to the ground.

They piled out of the vehicle and walked to their rooms. Eddie inserted a key, opening the door at the same time Carl opened his. He glanced at his friend. "I'll open the adjoining door."

Carl nodded as he stepped into the room.

Once inside, Eddie opened the interior access and caught a glimpse of Carl and Juan clearing their weapons and hiding them in a dresser drawer under some clothing. Both smiled as they walked into Eddie and Vinh's room.

"I'm hungry." Juan looked out the curtain.

Eddie slipped his gun into the nightstand drawer next to the Bible. "You guys want to order pizza?"

Carl smiled. "I want pineapple and ham on mine. And extra cheese, of course."

"Damn, don't you ever change it up?" Vinh asked

"Nope. It's bad luck to change things. Anyway, I don't trust the other toppings."

"Who doesn't trust pizza?" Vinh said.

"Like I said last time," Carl answered, "gives me the shits when they slip stuff in it. You know, when it's spicy. Unlike some around here, I stick with doing what I know is safe. Always know your capabilities. That's my motto in life."

He gave a sideways stare, long and hard, at Eddie.

But Eddie didn't even see. He was too busy watching Vinh as he dialed the pizza place.

After Vinh placed the order, he dropped the phone into the cradle and flopped on his bed. "Pizza will be here in twenty minutes. Now tell us what Mrs. Dang said."

Eddie pulled out the desk chair while Juan slid to the floor by the window and Carl sat on the edge of the bed. All eyes were on him.

"Okay, here is the short version." Eddie glanced around. "I told her how Dang killed Ray, slaughtered villagers, and stole their belongings. I even told her I'd been a captive of his." He rubbed his jaw. "She seemed surprised by some of the information I gave her."

Vinh rose to a sitting position. "Did you tell her about her son?"

Eddie frowned.

"I did. I told her that her husband executed their little boy."

"What did she say when you told her why?" Vinh asked.

"Didn't tell her that part." A deep furrow creased his forehead. "I guess I should've. Anyway, she wasn't happy. I think she believed me. I went on to tell her how he broke into my home and hurt Cheryl and killed my son."

Carl pursed his lips. "I bet that was a lot for her to digest."

"I believe so. But I also believe Mrs. Dang trusts me. She is supposed to be here at eight tonight."

Carl sprang up from the corner of the bed, eyes wide. "She's fucking what?" He stared at Eddie. "Coming here at eight. Straight to the room."

Eddie shrank. He had done it again, it seemed. He had gone and dropped the team right into harm's way without thinking. By not acting as a team. By doing what Carl said explicitly not to do.

That's what happens when you let a loose cannon get in charge, Carl's face seemed to say. He paced, running his hand across his chin.

"So, you're telling me you gave Dang's wife our location? Fuck me. You're more stupid than I ever gave you credit for, Eddie."

Eddie stood and pushed the curtain open.

He could take out Carl right now for using that tone, saying those words—calling him stupid. Hell, he already knew he was. But someone who was supposed to be an ally didn't say those kinds of things.

What the almighty fuck have I done? Dang's wife, here at eight. What was I thinking? For all I know, they could be on their way here now.

Eddie looked at his watch. "It's only four."

There was a knock at the door.

Everyone flinched.

Carl waved for everyone to go into the other room and lock the dividing door behind them. He knew they would keep their heads down.

Now he slid along the one empty wall that was free of furniture, alongside the bathroom, and peeped out through the spyhole in the door. A short Vietnamese teenager stood there, delivering the food they ordered. But it could equally have been a ruse.

"You got the order?" Carl shouted without opening the door.

"Got four pizzas and sodas," the young man said.

"What's on them?" Carl asked.

The young teen's face screwed up. "I think, cheese and ham . . . pineapple . . ." He strained to recall the rest.

Carl opened up, handed him the money, and then took the boxes.

"Keep the change."

"Thanks, man." The teenager turned on his heels, walking along the hall with a quick stride.

Carl looked in both directions of the hallway and then kicked the door closed. The guys emerged from room 208.

"Let's eat!" Vinh headed toward the pizza.

Carl set the boxes on the desk. "Don't think so. Eddie, you best get on the phone and sort out another pair of adjoining rooms for us. And get your bags packed, everyone. 'Cause we ain't staying here to get our brains blown out."

The message hit home.

Bags were packed, and Eddie got on the phone, landing them the pair of adjoining rooms down at the end of the hall where the peephole would overlook the corridor leading to rooms 206 and 208.

That way, when Mrs. Dang or her gun-toting posse arrived—if anyone even did—they could look out and see who it was.

•

The pizzas had long since gone cold, with a too-hard crust that almost required an immediate dental visit after eating it. The four friends sat in Eddie and Vinh's room, crunching away at their sorry dinner while Carl continued to glower at Eddie.

No one said anything. The atmosphere had changed.

It was one thing to help out a friend, but another when he nearly arranged to get you killed by being thoughtless, by defying all rules that governed operating as a team.

They washed their dried-out pizza down with Coke. Eddie's appetite seemed to have abandoned him; he ate only a half pizza and pushed the rest toward Vinh. "You can have that."

Vinh nodded.

Eddie noticed Juan pouring Jim Beam from his flask into his cup of Coke. "Hey man, you ought to slow down on that stuff." Eddie glared at Juan. "We don't know what tonight might bring."

"No worries. I drink like this all the time." Juan glared back. He was not about to change anything.

Carl shifted on the bed. Seeing friction between his buddies opened his eyes. "Okay, let's all relax. Let's save up the aggression for the bad guys."

Juan gulped a large portion of his drink.

"Well, pour me some." Eddie smiled, glad for Carl's softening.

Juan jumped to his feet and poured Eddie a healthy shot.

•

It wasn't long before Eddie glanced around and found his friends asleep. Loud snoring echoed from both rooms. He stood slowly and stepped over pizza boxes to the window. Eddie knew that any sudden movement or strange sound would wake the men in a heartbeat.

While he stared out the window, Eddie realized that this kind of waiting made it feel as if there was a knife twisting in his guts—or Canh beating him with the bamboo stick. Apprehension and fear tugged at him. He didn't know what information Mrs. Dang would bring to the meeting—or worse case, who she might bring with her; that was what Carl was worried might happen.

Without that knowledge, the waiting seemed to last an eternity.

He looked at his watch. Thirty more minutes until she should arrive. Eddie moved from the window into Carl's room. "Carl, time to get up. You need to go downstairs and signal me when she gets here."

As he rose to a sitting position, Carl felt upset not to be in charge as he rubbed the crust from his eyes. But of course, there was no point in Eddie being the one in the foyer, so Carl would have to do it.

"Heading to the lobby now." He reached into the drawer to retrieve his pistol and radio. "See you soon."

The room door closed behind him.

Eddie woke Juan and Vinh. "Let's go, guys. How about helping tidy up the room?" He started picking up boxes and cups.

"Give me everything and I'll take it to the trash in the hallway." Vinh reached for the boxes.

Juan opened the door while Eddie finished loading Vinh's outstretched arms. He left and returned in minutes.

"Okay, when she gets here, I want Juan to stay in his room. Vinh, you stay here with me. She knows you, and that might help when we let her in." Eddie peeked out the window.

When Eddie turned back to the room, he observed Juan taking another drink. "Damn Juan, knock that shit off, man."

Juan smiled and went into his room, closing the door behind him.

Eddie opened the door. "You want to talk about it?"

"Look, man, I know this is your gig. But I lost Bear, and I want the motherfucker to pay. And I mean, I want retribution." Juan threw a pillow across the room. "I'm way past the fucking denial stage. You got it?" He took another drink from the flask.

"I'm sorry, Juan." Eddie closed the door.

"What's that about?" Vinh whispered.

"Nothing, but let's keep an eye on him."

The radio's static crackled, then Carl's voice boomed, "Echo, she's heading upstairs now. She's alone."

"Roger that, Charlie. Stay there to see if anyone followed her," Eddie transmitted.

"Wilco," Carl said. The radios went silent.

There was a soft knock at the door.

Eddie peeked through the peephole and recognized Mrs. Dang. He looked all along the hallway. She stood in the hall, about to knock again on room 208's door. She wore khaki pants and a pale blue sweater that highlighted the color of her skin and petite figure.

As he stared, Eddie wondered how Dang got this attractive, classy woman to marry him.

Now, he cracked open the door then threw it wide. "Mrs. Dang," he called. "I am sorry, I got the room number wrong."

She looked down the corridor with surprise but seemed glad to see Eddie standing there—even if he was not quite where he was supposed to be. "Oh, okay." She started to walk down the hallway.

"I'm sorry about the mix-up. Come in." Eddie stood aside, swinging the door as wide as he could to welcome her.

As soon as she saw Vinh, she rushed toward him and placed her arms around his slender but muscular body. "How are you?" She released her grasp and placed a hand on his cheek. "Look at you, all grown up and such a handsome young man. I would recognize you anywhere." Her full lips pulled back into a smile, exposing white, even teeth.

His face turned crimson. "Thank you, Mrs. Dang. It's good to see you too." Vinh took a step backward.

"First off, everyone, please call me *Lài*."

She turned to face Eddie. "So, Eddie, what do you want from me?" Then she glanced toward Vinh as she wiped away a tear. "Vinh, what do you know about my son *Đức*?"

Eddie nodded at Vinh for him to speak first.

"I was with Duc when he died. Lieutenant Dang had a prisoner that escaped while he was gone. He got furious and blamed Duc and the old man." Vinh collapsed into the desk chair.

"Go ahead." Lai approached Vinh and put a hand on his shoulder.

Vinh's eyes darted around the room. "Lieutenant Dang made them kneel on the ground. Then he walked behind them. He stood there, rubbing the scar on his face. He had a habit of doing that." Vinh looked at the floor. "Then he pulled out his pistol and pointed at the back of the old man's head—he pulled the trigger. Lieutenant Dang did the same to Duc." He wiped his tears. "He even smiled while he stared at the bodies."

Lai sat on the end of the bed and took Vinh's hand. "Are you sure that's what happened?"

He looked up with a cold stare. "Yes, I'm sure. I'm positive that's what happened. I'll never forget it." He pulled his hand away. "He had Canh drag the bodies into the jungle."

Lai glared at Eddie. "What do you want from me?"

"I want to know when he will be alone at the warehouse or the union office." Eddie took several steps until he stood over her. "You understand what we aim to do, right?"

With her hand, she moved the hair that fell over her eyes. "Yes, I understand." Lai stared at Eddie. "How do I know you're strong enough to do it?"

Eddie's lips turned into a twisted smile. "Did he ever tell you how he got the scar on the right side of his face?"

"No, he didn't. Bao wouldn't talk about it."

"That's because I put it there ten years ago. Now, do you believe we're serious and capable?"

Silence filled the room.

Lai stood, looking out the window. Eddie could see her wipe at the tears streaming down her cheek. She crossed her arms as she stared at the night sky. He believed she was a good woman, a person with a conscience.

She turned to face Eddie, dropping her arms to her side.

"He's at Seadrift right now. In two days, he will be at the warehouse at seven in the morning." Her lips pointed downward with sadness radiating from her eyes. "And you want to know about Canh too?"

"Yes, we need to find them both." Eddie was not as brave or as bold as Carl—he couldn't simply say *kill them both*.

Maybe he should have asked Carl to head up to the room too, in case of any mixed messages. But Lai answered the question Eddie had posed.

"My husband told me that Canh works in the warehouse most nights, from nine to eleven. Do you need anything else?"

"Yes, can you make sure the side door is left unlocked when your husband goes to work that morning?"

"Yes," she said meekly, as if Eddie had asked her to water his plants for him while he was away. "I can do that. And that's all?" Lai looked scared. "You won't ask me to do anything else? Because I need to know now, if there's more . . . Because I can't do more."

Eddie opened the door. "No, ma'am, there is no more. That's it. I won't ask you to do anything else. You've been most helpful."

She tried to smile as she walked out of the room.

As Lai strode along the carpeted corridor, Eddie looked in both directions to determine if anyone was watching.

A FIGHT AT THE WAREHOUSE

After Carl returned to the room, he stuck his head through the doorway. "How did it go?"

"I think she's with us." Eddie smiled. "She took the news about her son hard, but I think deep down, she always knew. And we have his schedule—the day after tomorrow is the day."

"Good ally to have, for sure." Carl rubbed his eyes. "Juan's asleep."

"Hey, do you know what's eating at Juan? He seems off his game." Eddie stood, searching Carl's eyes for an answer.

"He hasn't confided in me, but he did tell me he's been drinking a lot. I think all this has brought back memories of Bear's death. You know how close they were. Probably wants to make sure he gets a piece of Dang before you do." Carl chuckled. "Does that make sense?"

"Yeah, it does. I'm starting to worry about him. That's all."

"Understand. I'm hitting the sack. See you in the morning." Carl closed the door.

Eddie looked over at Vinh—he was already asleep.

When he flopped on his bed, Eddie couldn't focus on a single thought because of the nervous anticipation that ran through his body. Even his feet tingled with excitement. Yet he knew he had to get through another day before he could go to the warehouse.

He could picture shooting Dang in the head, executing him like Dang had executed Ray.

It wasn't long before he nodded off with a smile on his face. And a smile was rare to see on him these days.

•

Unknown to Eddie, when everyone was asleep, Juan quietly rose from his bed, unlocked the motel room door, and slipped out, carrying his pistol. After he slid behind the wheel of the Mazda, he cranked the vehicle and headed in the direction of Little Saigon. Along the way, Juan stopped at a liquor store and purchased a pint of Jim Beam.

Back at the car, he opened the bottle and took a long swig.

During the drive, he rolled the window down, allowing the crisp night air to drift against his body. He took another gulp from the bottle. His destination, of course, was the warehouse.

As he pulled into the same parking spot by the big tree, Juan searched for anyone that might be lingering in the area. It looked empty.

He hid the keys between the visor and roof, leaving the car unlocked, then stuffed the pint bottle of Jim Beam into his back pocket.

The warehouse was only a short walk from the parking lot.

Along the sidewalk, he found few shoppers or tourists. The area appeared deserted—most of the shops and restaurants were already closed for the night.

When he approached the warehouse, Juan spotted a light through the front window; he shifted the pistol from his waistband to the sweater pocket, then flipped the hood over his head. He took short, careful steps as he neared the side entrance.

He stopped and placed an ear against the door.

Vietnamese music, a confusing stream of emotionally charged sounds, flowed from the building.

Juan slowly turned the handle and, to his amazement, found the entrance unlocked. He pulled the heavy windowless door open several inches, attempting to get a view of the area. The music was louder now. As his eyes scanned from the back of the darkened room to the front, he froze. A man sat in a chair behind a desk, shuffling papers under the single light that shone in the entire vast space.

After he slid through the open door, Juan slowly eased it closed, releasing the handle so the man wouldn't hear the click of the latch. Juan stood in the shadows, letting his eyes slowly adjust to the light and darkness of the room. He crept to the far wall where it was darker, and then followed along with the structure toward the man while staying in the shadows.

The chair squeaked, and the man said over his shoulder, "Mister *Đặng*." He turned and looked toward the side door and didn't see anyone.

Juan slid lower to the floor—the darkness concealing him from view. The man turned back to his work. Juan began creeping forward until the darkness would no longer hide him. He stood straight, charging the man.

The man rolled his chair back as he grabbed the bamboo stick. He stood, facing the sound. "What do you want?" he yelled. Then he swung the weapon at Juan's head.

Juan ducked as the stick zoomed overhead—he felt the breeze from the force of the blow it would've delivered. Once he regained his footing, Juan threw a wild overhand right fist that connected with the left side of the man's head. Juan winced from the pain that shot up his arm. The man took several steps backward from the force of the blow, but still held onto the stick.

Then Juan recognized the man. "Canh. You son of a bitch."

Canh shook his head, taking a defensive position while holding out the stick. "How do you know me?"

"You and your boss killed my best friend in Vietnam." Juan's lips twisted upwards as his eyes turned cold. "Now it's your turn."

Without warning, Canh rushed forward, striking Juan across the ribs with the bamboo stick. Juan fell to the ground, grabbing his left side. The glass from the broken bottle in his pocket pierced the skin of his right butt cheek. Bourbon soaked his clothes and ran onto the floor, mixing with his blood. A loud groan escaped from between his clenched teeth as he lay prostrate and injured on the floor.

Canh smiled and delivered another blow to his adversary, but Juan rolled to his right to avoid the stick. It thudded into the concrete, making a loud slapping sound that echoed through the building. When he jumped to his feet, Juan let go of his injured side and pulled the pistol from his sweater pocket. He pointed the gun at Canh. "Now you're gonna die, motherfucker." Juan squeezed the trigger. It sounded like a cannon firing in the small confines of the warehouse.

The bullet hit Canh, spinning him to the left, and then he collapsed on the floor with the stick still in his right hand.

He didn't move or make another sound.

Carefully, Juan approached Canh, not sure where the bullet had struck.

He kicked his feet, no movement.

Then he kicked him on the right side, nothing.

With a smile tugging at his lips, Juan pointed the pistol at Canh's head for the kill shot.

Before Juan knew what happened, Canh slid the stick between Juan's legs and twisted hard, flipping him to the floor. Juan's head thudded on the concrete, sending blood streaming from the wound. His pistol skidded across the dirty surface.

Canh stood over Juan with blood running down his shirt from the wound in his shoulder. "You've made a big mistake, little man."

Juan looked up with glassy eyes. "Fuck you, motherfucker."

The stick hit Juan across the head with full force, cracking his skull. Juan's eyes fluttered, his hands trembled, his body shook, and then he was still. His eyes rolled back while blood foamed from his mouth.

Canh stared down at Juan and kicked him hard on the left side. He walked to his desk and picked up the telephone handset from the cradle, then dialed a number.

•

Carl busted into the room. "Eddie, wake up. Juan is gone."

Eddie rolled over.

"What do you mean, gone? You sure he isn't out getting breakfast? You know how he's hungry all the time. He's as bad as Vinh."

"No, he's gone. His pistol and car are gone too." Carl wiped his face. "Vinh, get up." He kicked the legs of Vinh's bed.

Eddie slid out of bed. "Let's think this through before we do anything rash. We don't want to piss Juan off. He's not too happy with me as it is."

Vinh rolled out of bed and turned on the television.

"I don't know how he got out of the room without me knowing," Carl said, staring out the window.

"It's not your fault." Eddie rested his hand on Carl's shoulder. "You aren't the guy's babysitter."

"Hey fellas, quiet down, listen to this."

Vinh waved for them to pay attention.

They stopped talking and stared at the television.

The news anchor reported, "Early this morning, the body of a Hispanic male, thirty to thirty-five years old, was found in an alley near Little Saigon. The reports we've received allege he was beaten to death with a heavy, blunt weapon like a bat or heavy stick. The police said the man smelled of alcohol. We'll post more details as they come in. Stay tuned for the weather . . ."

"Turn that shit off." Eddie paced the room. "What in the fuck did he get himself into? You know they're talking about Juan." He took a breath. "And it had to be Canh that beat him. Only one man that I know of can do that much damage with a blunt stick."

Eddie glanced around the room. The numbness of hearing the news slowly faded away. He gasped for air, but it seemed nothing came into his lungs. In desperation, he sucked in another breath that burned his insides.

His eyes welled with tears as he stared out into the darkness of the early morning. The realization dawned on him. Juan was dead. Nothing he could do would change that. He gave one final sigh before looking at the other two men in the room.

And what was worse, they had no idea how all this came to pass.

If Juan had gone looking for Dang, then he had put the enemy on alert. Now there were additional complications.

"We can't go to the police or even try to identify that it's Juan." Carl sat at the end of the bed. "Hell, he could've killed someone for all we know. Then we're all in it together."

Eddie stared out the window. "Damn, what a mess. I agree with you, Carl. We can't do anything for Juan now. Let the police handle it, and they'll contact his family too." He turned to face his two friends. "We'll stay low today and try to get Dang tomorrow morning."

Carl reached for the adjoining door.

"Let's go and see if we can find where he left the car."

Eddie turned away from the window. "Okay, let's go downstairs." He reached into the nightstand and removed the pistol. "Everyone bring your radio and gun, just in case." He tucked the .45 into the waistband of his jeans.

NOTHING TO DO BUT WAIT

The three men strode to where the van was parked. Carl opened the driver door and slid behind the wheel while Vinh piled into the rear and Eddie climbed into the passenger seat. Once the doors slammed closed, Carl drove toward the frontage road.

Carl shifted in his seat to face Eddie. "I'm going to the parking lot off the main drag. I bet the car is there."

"You're probably right." Eddie turned to stare out the window.

The men were quiet during the ride to Little Saigon.

As the van maneuvered through traffic, Eddie thought of Juan. He had grieved so many times over the years—for his parents, the loss of friends, brothers in arms, and his son, Ray. At this moment, his heart felt empty, believing that Juan had probably died alone and that Canh had dumped him in the alley. Tears welled in his eyes. Eddie turned to watch the traffic and the buildings flash by as the car rolled along the road.

It seemed like only seconds had passed when Carl said, "We're here."

Eddie snapped out of his semi-hypnotic state as the vehicle coasted to a stop in the parking lot. "There's his car."

The three men strode toward the red Mazda.

Carl opened the driver's door and surveyed the interior. "Juan left the door unlocked." He reached overhead, pulling the visor down. A set of keys fell onto the floorboard. "Here are the keys."

"Anything else?" Vinh asked.

"Found something." Carl held up a photo album. "I'll throw it in the van."

Eddie looked over Carl's shoulder.

"Damn, it was like he didn't expect to come back to the car." He stepped back, shaking his head. "Let's go get some breakfast."

For a moment, Eddie realized his actions were the same as when he'd been in Vietnam. A brother got killed, and you'd say, "It don't mean nothin'" and then sit down to eat your C-rations.

What a fucked-up world we live in.

Vinh slapped Eddie on the back.

"Want to eat at the place where we had lunch yesterday?"

"Good idea. Let's go."

Eddie followed Vinh and Carl as they went to the restaurant a block away. He understood that he kept his feelings in the middle of the road most times. Not too low, not too high. Even after a devastating event like Juan getting killed, he was amazed at how quickly he slipped right back into that middle zone. Eddie often wondered how long he could continue living like that.

At the restaurant, they pulled chairs out at a table by the front window.

The same waitress as the day before stopped by their table.

"So, you're here again!" Her eyes twinkled. "Our food must be good. You even brought a friend with you." This time she wore a *áo dài* and had her long hair pulled into a bun.

"You got us pegged." Eddie chuckled. "I'll have a cup of coffee and two banh mi sandwiches."

"Two? You must be hungry." She turned her attention to Carl. "And you, sir?"

Carl sat straighter in the chair. "I'll have the same." He glanced at Eddie. "It's good, right?"

"You bet." Eddie's eyes lit up. "I thought so, anyway." It'd be spicy, but Eddie omitted that part.

She looked at Vinh. "What about you, young man?"

Vinh picked at something on his sweater, and then looked up. "I'll have the same but a Coke instead of coffee."

"You got it." Before she walked away, she said, "I'll be back with the drinks." She quickly disappeared into the kitchen.

After the waitress served the meal, the three men ate in silence. Eddie would take a bite and then stare out the window, watching people coming and going.

The crowds started to grow larger as the morning sun rose higher in the clear blue sky. There were as many tourists on the streets as there were locals.

"Eddie, get up and leave the table now," Carl whispered.

Without questioning, Eddie stood, pulled his hat down, and walked toward the restrooms.

Carl kicked Vinh under the table. "Hold your head down by my side."

Vinh did as requested. "What's going on?" he muttered.

"Canh was coming toward us, and now he's stopped outside the restaurant, about ten feet from us."

Carl shifted his massive frame to conceal Vinh better.

While Carl took a bite of his sandwich, Canh glanced in the restaurant window. He stood and stared for a moment.

Carl noticed that Canh's left arm was in a sling.

Out of nowhere, Lai appeared.

She pointed down the street as she spoke to Canh. When Canh and Lai walked toward the union office, she gave Carl a quick smile.

Carl made eye contact with her and turned his hand in an unnoticeable wave. She nodded at him.

"He's gone." Carl nudged Vinh. "How about getting Eddie?"

Vinh walked back to the bathroom and returned with Eddie a minute later.

Eddie wiped his forehead. "Vinh said Canh was standing outside the window?"

"He was. But Lai ran over and convinced him to start walking." Carl looked out the window. "Man, she probably saved our ass. It's a good thing he's never seen me before." He felt his pocket. "Damn,

I wish I'd never quit smoking." Carl picked up his cup. "He had his left arm in a sling. I bet Juan shot his ass."

Once they finished the meal, they decided to go back to the hotel.

The drive was a little longer because of the traffic. Carl parked the van and they jumped out to stretch their legs.

Eddie slammed the car door. "Hell, let's go to the room and get some rest." Eddie looked at his watch. "After a nap, let's get the weapons cleaned and the equipment ready for tomorrow."

Carl was already taking long strides to the room. "Damn, spicy food. I don't know if I'll make it in time."

"What about dinner?" Vinh asked. "That's what I'm thinking about."

"Damn, Vinh, we just ate." Eddie laughed.

Carl slapped Vinh on the back. "Like the boy says, let's eat again. Why not? Shit, let's go to the steak place down the road. Might be our last meal." Carl's tune had changed from earlier. Losing a team member had united them.

Eddie grinned at Carl. "You better hurry."

"See you later," Carl yelled over his shoulder as he ran through the motel front door.

The three men fell asleep in no time.

•

After a hardy steak meal, the men walked back to the motel. They joked and laughed as if they were going home from a Saturday night out.

A short distance from the motel, Eddie put his arms around both men. "We don't know what tomorrow will bring, so let's get some sleep. I think we should get up early and be outside the warehouse before six-thirty." He walked backward for a moment. "That should give us time to be ready when Dang arrives. What d'you say, boss?"

He turned to seek Carl's approval.

"I'm good with that. Stick to the plan this time."

No more was said on the matter. The group stopped at the motel entrance and sat on the bench near the door.

Carl surveyed his surroundings. "I'll stay outside to take care of anyone that attempts to go through the front door of the warehouse after you're inside." Then he glanced at the others. "Vinh, you guard the side door." Eddie sat staring at the night sky. "Eddie, go in alone."

"Whatever you say." Vinh sprang to his feet. "Sounds like a plan."

Carl and Eddie stood and strolled toward the entrance.

•

Eddie whimpered in his sleep, "Ray, follow me!" and then flipped onto his stomach, struggling to get out of the bed. "Let's go, Ray."

When Eddie turned onto his side, he yelled, "Run, it's fucking Dang!"

He watched Laurel stare into the barrel of the pistol.

Eddie's heart beat hard against his chest.

"I'm going to kill you!" he screamed at Dang.

"Eddie, it's okay." Vinh shook his arm. "It's a dream, man. You're okay."

Eddie slid out of bed, looking around the room. "What time is it?" He felt embarrassed that Vinh had witnessed his nightmare.

Vinh checked his watch. "It's four-thirty."

"Shit, might as well get up. I'll put some coffee on." Eddie walked to the sink to fill the container with water. He poured it into the coffee maker and turned it on. "Hope it doesn't take too long."

He stood at the window, staring into the dark but starlit early morning sky, holding a pistol in his hand. Eddie eyed the weapon, understanding what this day would bring. His steady hand lifted the gun to shoulder-height while he aimed at an imaginary target.

The target wasn't really imaginary, though. It was Dang. He nodded at the reflection in the window. He was ready.

The strong aroma of brewed coffee snapped Eddie from his trance. "You want some?" he offered Vinh as he filled a cup.

"Thanks." Vinh took the hot, dark liquid.

Carl walked into the room carrying donuts. "I thought I smelled coffee."

"Hey, a good morning would be nice, you guys." Eddie laughed as he handed Carl a cup.

Vinh and Carl sat quietly, enjoying the smell and flavor of their morning drinks. They stuffed one donut after another into their mouths, washing it all down with coffee.

Eddie went back to the window and stared outside, deep in thought. He enjoyed the quiet of the early morning hours, but every time he thought of Dang his blood boiled and he had to fight to keep his anger under control because he knew blind hatred might get him and his friends killed.

At least he'd learned something from earlier rash mistakes.

It wasn't only the anger, though, that was troubling him. At times, he doubted his ability to physically kill Dang, or mentally outsmart him. Eddie knew he was a good soldier—he always felt he had more than what it took to be one.

His confidence surged with the memory of escaping from Dang, not once, but twice, holding him down while cutting his face and now tracking him to the place he worked and lived. Eddie stood straighter, knowing he could do this.

Before he turned away from the window, he thought of calling Cheryl but decided to wait.

"Okay, guys, let's load up and head to Little Saigon. We got a date." Eddie shot Carl a glance. "How about another one of those donuts?"

Vinh and Carl laughed.

"Take all you want." Carl threw the box at Eddie.

Eddie caught it, pulled out a donut, and chowed down. Then he shouldered his bag.

Carl turned the door handle. "Let's do it."

The three friends took long strides through the front entrance toward the van. Once everyone was seated, Carl turned the ignition and the engine came alive with a roar. The van shuddered when he put it into gear and pressed the accelerator. "Sure hope this ol' girl holds up until we get home," Carl chuckled.

AT LAST, A MEETING

Without morning traffic, they made good time to the parking lot. Carl wheeled the van into the same parking spot by the big tree.

The Mazda was still parked nearby. He switched the ignition off and turned to face Eddie and Vinh.

Eddie rolled down the window, allowing the fresh morning air to circulate in the van.

"Okay, one more time." Carl's face turned serious. "I'm going to wait outside near the front entrance to watch for anyone attempting to enter the building. I'll do whatever I need to do. I know you and Vinh don't need any surprises." He smiled. "You'll head in via the side door, Eddie, and Vinh will stay outside to guard that same door, okay? Lai said she'd leave it unlocked. Hopefully, you'll be in and out within a couple of minutes."

Carl's eyes narrowed.

"The question then is, what do we do afterward? What do you reckon, Eddie?" He made a point of directly asking Eddie for an opinion, figuring that he'd got stuck with the planning. Eddie needed at least some element of being in control. And besides, the more Eddie thought about the finer points, the better—and the less likely he was to go off on his own.

But, as usual, Eddie's response was not as focused as Carl would've liked.

"Shit, let's get back to the van and the hell away from here." Eddie rubbed his jaw as he scanned the parking area.

He laughed and checked his watch.

Carl did the same.

"Okay, it's six-thirty. Let's head to the building and get eyes on."

The three men scrambled out of the van. Eddie gazed at the dark, early morning sky and smiled at the full moon.

Carl quietly closed the driver's door. "I put the keys under the visor like Juan did, in case I don't make it back."

Eddie's brows drew together.

"We're all coming back." He slapped Carl on the back. "Let's do a quick radio check." Each man pushed the talk button to listen to the squelching sound on the other radios. "Good to go."

Carl led the way, taking long strides as Vinh and Eddie followed one behind the other. There weren't any pedestrians on the sidewalk, and few vehicles traveled the road. They crossed the street in front of the warehouse at a diagonal, then followed the bushes along the driveway on the opposite side of the building.

The three men knelt behind the bushes, hiding in the shadows as they watched the side door for signs of movement.

Eddie saw the light shining through the window. Then he observed what he believed were two—maybe three—figures moving about the room.

As he watched the shadows through the window, his heart thumped in his chest, banging like it was struggling to get out. He crouched higher for a better view and his legs trembled as if his weight was too much to lift. Eddie started to inhale and exhale slowly to calm his body.

He needed his mind sharp and his body ready to carry out the mission.

Carl touched Eddie's shoulder. "I see them. I'm going to the front of the building. I'll keep low and send one squelch if I stop someone and two if they're coming into the building."

Eddie almost stood to see better over the bushes.

"Got it." Eddie watched as Carl bent low and scuttled toward the street.

"Vinh, move to cover the door after I enter the building," Eddie whispered. "Going now."

He crept toward the closed door. Eddie's hands trembled as he went, and his eyes watered as he reached for the door handle. He knew something evil was behind it. Sweat started to run down his body as his damp hand pushed the handle, freeing the latch. It was unlocked. Lai had kept her promise.

With his right hand, Eddie removed the pistol while placing his finger into the trigger housing. His breathing grew faster as he pulled the door open just enough so he could slide into the room. Everything was silent—only a few light bulbs shone in the large room.

•

Out front, Carl saw the heavyset Vietnamese man favoring his left arm as he crossed the road toward the warehouse. Once the man stepped onto the sidewalk, Carl acted as if he was looking for a cigarette.

"Excuse me, you got a light?"

The man stopped, staring at Carl. "No." He scowled and pointed down the street. "You need to move away from here."

"I don't think so." Carl opened his sweater, exposing the pistol in the waistband of his jeans. "Now, move toward me, slowly."

Carl put his hand on the handle of the gun.

The man's eyes went wide. "Do you know who I work for?" He reached inside his jacket.

"Yes, I do." Before the man could say another word, Carl had the pistol pressed against his stomach. "I'll take that." He removed the man's gun. "Now, you're gonna come with me and act friendly."

The man glared. "No, I'm not going anywhere with you."

Within a second, the man was wincing in pain as Carl's thumb pressed into his left shoulder. His face turned pale and then his knees buckled from under him.

Carl pushed the man forward. "Go to that large tree in front of the building."

The heavyset man stumbled under the large limbs of the live oak and leaned against the massive tree trunk. The branches concealed the men from the sidewalk and road.

Carl's face contorted to something different, almost evil.

"So, I take it you're the fat slob that held my friend's wife when Canh hit her, killing their son."

"How do you know this?" the man asked.

Carl laughed. "You can ask your boss in about ten minutes."

Without thinking, Carl swung the butt of the pistol into the side of the man's head with the entire force of his two hundred pounds. When it struck the Vietnamese man's skull, a soft groan escaped the man's lips and he fell to the ground.

Carl bent over the body and checked his pulse. "Fuck, he's dead."

•

Back at the warehouse, Eddie closed the door, releasing the handle slowly. He took slow, cautious steps toward the front of the building where the three people stood. It was Lai, Canh, and Dang.

He saw Lai glance his way.

Eddie froze for a moment, waiting for her to cry out. She said nothing and calmly returned her gaze to the front of the building.

CHAPTER 25

SOMEONE WILL DIE

Canh stood quickly, grabbing his stick. "*Nguyễn*, is that you?" His eyes darted in Eddie's direction.

As he pointed his pistol, Eddie said, "No, it's not." He covered the ground quickly between the door and the desk. "Drop the fucking stick, Canh." Eddie stood no more than ten feet from the group.

With a twisted smile, Dang turned as if he had all day to face Eddie. "So good to see you again, Sergeant Henderson." He smoothed his hair.

Eddie ignored Dang. "Ma'am, could you step away from the desk, please?" Eddie pointed at an area near the front door.

Lai nodded and walked toward the wall.

Eddie noticed Dang's right arm twitch.

Within seconds, Canh charged, swinging the stick at Eddie's head.

He ducked and rolled to his right side. As Eddie bounced to his feet, Canh attempted an off-balance swing at Eddie's ribs.

Before the stick arrived, Eddie moved in close, delivering a kick to Canh's balls. He yelled in pain, bending over and grabbing at his manhood.

Eddie then thrust his right knee into the face of the attacker, smashing his nose and sending blood spurting into the air.

Canh fell to the ground with his knees pulled to his chest, whimpering.

Eddie swung his right hand and aimed the pistol at Canh's head. "Now you die, you son of a bitch."

A gun cocked behind him. "Stop." Dang pressed the pistol against Eddie's head. "Drop your weapon."

After a moment of hesitation, Eddie lowered the pistol.

"Lai, come and get his gun," Dang ordered.

She moved slowly toward Eddie.

Dang glared at her. "Move faster."

When she reached Eddie, she grasped the weapon with both hands. She let her fingers touch his hand but didn't look into his eyes.

"Give it to me." Dang snatched the pistol from her. "Now, stand by the desk." He slid the gun into the waistband of his pants.

Eddie started to turn around, but Dang pushed the pistol harder against his head.

"Stop. Drop to your knees."

As he started to bend downward, Eddie rotated on the balls of his feet to face Dang while grabbing his right wrist. With a hard downward twist the pistol fell to the floor with a loud clanking noise.

Dang grunted, surprised by Eddie's quick move to disarm him. He deftly rotated his arm while following the movement caused by Eddie's momentum. Then Dang jerked free from Eddie's grasp.

As he stared at Eddie, Dang wiped at the sweat running down his face. His lips curled baring his teeth.

Eddie took up a fighting stance, circling to Dang's left. His veins pulsed in his neck as he glared at Dang.

He stepped forward throwing a left jab that Dang blocked. Dang flashed a tight-lipped smile as he glowered at Eddie.

Shifting his weight forward, Eddie threw a right cross with all his strength behind the punch. When his fist connected, he felt a sense of pleasure.

Dang staggered, blood oozing from the cut high on his left cheek. His eyes glazed over as his knees started to buckle.

When Eddie saw him waver, he knocked him to the ground with an open handed punch to the sternum. Before he realized it, he was sitting on Dang's chest with his hands around Dang's throat.

He squeezed hard, wanting to prevent the much needed oxygen from entering Dang's body. The years of hatred exploded inside Eddie. He knew that, at last, he was going to kill Dang with his bare hands. Eddie's eyes narrowed, focused.

Then Eddie noticed Dang's eyes fixated on something behind him. The hair on Eddie's neck stood on end, but it was too late.

Dang's lips twisted into a sneer.

The blow from the bamboo stick struck Eddie across the shoulders, knocking him to the concrete floor. Waves of pain coursed through his body. While on his back, his eyes began to focus. He saw Canh standing over him with the stick raised above his head.

He drew his right leg into his chest. With all the force he could muster, Eddie slammed his foot into Canh's groin area.

Canh fell to the floor squealing like a pig.

Dang jammed the pistol barrel hard against Eddie's skull. "Now get on your fucking knees."

Eddie complied with his order, and Dang stepped in front of him, still holding him at gunpoint.

"Put your hands behind your head."

Canh attempted to stand but groaned and fell back to the concrete floor.

Eddie's eyes darted around the room, searching for a way out. He didn't see one, and he knew that no one would come into the building unless he sent the signal.

Dang gazed down at his prisoner. "This is like old times. I told you that you were mine." The pupils of his eyes turned red. "Too bad about your friend. He didn't have the strength to survive." He reached into his pocket and removed a photograph. "Your wife is so beautiful." He flipped it so Eddie could see the image, then slid it in his pocket.

Eddie started to stand. "Fuck you, motherfucker."

Dang cuffed him against the neck with the barrel of the pistol.

"I told you not to move."

Eddie winced in pain from the blow as his knees found the concrete floor.

"Now, you're going to die." Dang pointed the pistol at the center of Eddie's forehead and winked. "For my son."

Eddie couldn't breathe; it felt like something sucked all the oxygen from the room. His heart raced because he was running out of time for the guys to save him. He couldn't even force a cry for help. Eddie understood this was the end for him. He needed to accept it—to die like a man.

"Stop!" Lai walked between Eddie and her husband. "Let me do it." Her full lips pulled back into a smile. "I want revenge for my son. Bao, give me the gun." She stretched her arm out, reaching for the weapon.

Eddie's mouth dropped open.

Looking confused but impressed, Dang handed his wife the pistol.

"I'm proud of you."

With the weapon in hand, she stepped next to her husband. She raised her right arm, aiming at Eddie.

He shook his head and then closed his eyes.

Betrayal. Disappointment.

That was what he felt as Lai wielded a weapon with which she intended to kill him.

Dang had her brainwashed.

That much was clear.

He thought of Cheryl, Mitch, and Ronnie and the love he had for them. Eddie had wanted to be a perfect husband and father, and it bothered him that he'd been neither. It was hard to move past his mistakes. He would do the same stupid things over and over, but at least he owned every mistake he had made. Especially now.

And this—this was the biggest one yet.

His last thought was that he hoped Cheryl would still love him—that she wouldn't hate him for leaving her and the kids.

A tear ran down his cheek.

The sound of a pistol firing exploded in the air. Then the gun discharged again, the sounds reverberating in the empty warehouse.

The smell of gun smoke burnt Eddie's nostrils and the lining of his lungs.

He had been close to death several times before today. But this, now, was different. Men who had been near to death then saved described all this perfectly. They said injuries hurt and were mired in pain and screaming, but that death came silently and was painless.

Still, he wondered how a bullet in the head could possibly be so free of suffering. Before him on the floor was an oozing lake of red, accompanied by a familiar smell, the tang of iron and brain fragments. Both this sight and smell had assaulted his senses so many times before. And so it was done then. He waited to fade, waited for the sight to ebb slowly away, his hearing the last thing to leave him, like other men had described.

He waited.

•

At the sound of the shots, Vinh burst through the side door and Carl ran in through the front. Both men stopped in their tracks.

Eddie opened his eyes, tears blurring and stinging his vision. His ears were still ringing.

There stood Lai with her arms at her side, a pistol in her right hand.

She held the pose, as if frozen in shock and horror.

Eddie saw Dang with the side of his skull missing, his brains gone too—a dark, purplish mass visible on the far side of his partially vacated head. He lay motionless in a pool of blood, with his body spread in a bizarre position, one heel up by the back of his knee and the second leg out at an awkward angle.

Eddie's gaze then fell on Canh, who had a large hole in his forehead.

"Thank you." Eddie stood, staring into Lai's eyes.

When she dropped the pistol, the metallic sound echoed in the room. "You didn't deserve to die." Lai wiped away a tear. "He was an evil man that was going to kill a good person. Like he killed so many."

Eddie took quick steps to her.

"I don't know how to repay you." He embraced her. She writhed and struggled, making Eddie pull back.

"You don't need to repay me. Just go." Lai pushed him away even further. "Go on. I'll tell the police that a rival gang shot Canh and Bao . . . I'll think of something. Go."

Carl faced Lai. "The big guy is dead too. He's under the tree out front." He grabbed Eddie by the arm. "Like she said. We need to go. Now!"

"Wait a minute." Eddie reached into Dang's shirt pocket and removed the photograph.

He looked at Cheryl and put the picture into his pocket.

"I always wondered where that picture came from." Lai gazed at him, calmer now. "I wondered . . . you know . . ."

Eddie barely dared touch her arm, but did it anyway.

"You assumed he was having an affair?" Eddie asked. "No. It's my wife, Cheryl, on our wedding day ten years ago."

He picked up his pistol, turned, and ran with Carl toward Vinh. The three men slipped out the side door and disappeared into the streets of Little Saigon.

A QUIET DRIVE HOME

On the drive back to the motel, the men were silent. There were no celebratory shouts of happiness or clinks of bourbon glasses raised in endless toasts. There was nothing. They'd experienced death before and knew not to celebrate it—not even people as evil or as cruel as Dang and Canh, men who deserved to die.

"I want to go home to Cheryl now," Eddie said, as if anyone was still listening—they were all too deeply embedded in their thoughts.

But the men nodded. Yet, they did not head back to Eddie's place. They had to see the plan through—to the end.

"We got a plan, Eddie." Carl looked across at him.

"Yeah. I know."

They returned to the motel to spend a final night. That way, when the cops were asking around at the local hotels, no clerk could say that four men booked in for two nights and went away right after the killings.

But still, it's lousy not to see Cheryl tonight.

Then he realized he could.

As Carl drove on, Eddie fumbled in his pocket and pulled out the photo Dang had kindly delivered back to him. "Thanks, Dang."

In the late morning, after a last sleep at the motel, the men grabbed their weapons and bags, heading to the front desk. The desk clerk was an older, heavyset woman dressed in a rumpled pants suit. It appeared that she'd rolled out of bed ten minutes ago.

While Eddie stood at the counter, he reminded himself to use the same name he checked in with. "I'm checking out, last name of Robinson." They had already settled for 206 and 208, the rooms they'd moved from earlier.

The woman slowly searched for the bill.

She handed it to Eddie. "Cash or charge?"

"Cash, please." Eddie pulled the bills from his pocket and counted them out on the counter. "That should cover it."

"Yes, it does. I hope you enjoyed your stay," the woman said, not looking up as she stuffed the money into the drawer. And they set off for home—heading back in the direction of Eddie and Cheryl's.

It was a long and boring drive.

They finished the job, every task ticked off, and the atmosphere should have been happy. But it was not—it was flat. Hearts and minds appeared broken, somehow. Killing men was never a good feeling—or maybe the good feeling lasted only a few minutes, till the adrenaline wore off, and then the quiet reflection and the replays kicked in. Seeing men's brains splashed about and having to watch a woman kill her husband, knowing her life would never be the same . . . It was not the best.

Vinh had gone off his food now. That was the most significant indication that they had a lot to process. "I'll have a coffee when we stop." Yet they looked at the restaurants as they drove by and still didn't stop.

Eddie stared ceaselessly at the picture of Cheryl, thinking how odd it seemed that he still loved holding the photograph in his hands despite knowing where it had been all these years, tucked in close against the skin of his worst enemy.

With the roar of the engine becoming bothersome, Eddie turned on the radio and adjusted the volume. Music reverberated throughout the van.

After ten minutes of music, the news began. "At the top of the hour—the Houston Police Department identified the man found murdered in an alley in the Little Saigon district. He is Juan Jackson who resides in San Antonio. There are no suspects at this time. Please stay tuned for the weather . . ."

Without a word, Eddie turned the radio off.

The three men remained deep in thought.

Carl stared straight ahead, his hands firmly on the wheel, looking as calm and in control as ever, while his mind whirred.

Now and then, he turned to check on his two buddies.

"Everyone okay?" he asked.

"All okay," they said.

CHAPTER 27

THE TELEPHONE CALL

When the van finally came to a stop in front of Eddie's house the three friends sat and stared at the street, not especially eager to get out. Travel was something of a leveler. Reality was about to hit home.

They were beat, exhausted, miserable. And silent. More than anything, memories of Juan flashed before Eddie. He recalled his humor, his friendship, and his abilities in battle. Juan hadn't deserved to die—he missed him already.

But Juan had also taught Eddie a lot. He could've been where Juan was now if Carl hadn't reined him in. With a cramped, tired body, Eddie climbed from the van. He stood for a moment, taking in the neighborhood, the peacefulness of it all. "Come on, guys, let's go inside." He led the way toward the front door at a slow pace, dragging his feet on the concrete sidewalk.

Once inside, Eddie smiled, knowing he was home. The familiar surroundings and smells welcomed him. His eyes twinkled with the image of the boys running through the living room to welcome him back.

When he walked around the sofa, though, he recalled the bullet holes in the wall, Cheryl lying on the floor crying, the blood that pooled beside her. And he saw Dang's evil smile, and those glowing red demonic eyes.

He acknowledged that Dang's and Canh's deaths were necessary, and he felt no remorse for the demise of the two ex-Viet Cong soldiers. Even though it wasn't by his own hands, literally speaking, he understood that he had played a pivotal part in their deaths. In his heart, Eddie knew, given a chance, he could've pulled the trigger both times without a second thought.

He stepped over the spot where baby Ray had died, heading to the bedroom to put his gear away. When Eddie walked down the hallway toward the living room, he noticed Vinh sitting on the bed with his head in his hands.

Carl stepped into the room too, passing without a word spoken, and sprawled across Mitch's bed.

After Eddie made his way to the kitchen, he fixed a Jim Beam and Coke, set the glass on the table, and reached for the telephone. While dialing the number, he took a long sip of the drink. The phone rang.

"Hello," Cheryl answered.

"Cheryl, I'm home." Eddie smiled as he looked out the window. "I can't even tell you how much I love you." He took another drink. "I've missed you and the boys. I can't wait for you to come home."

Tears wet his eyes.

"I didn't think you would ever call." Her voice trembled. "Waiting to hear you're okay . . . It was so horrible." She paused. "I love you. Are you alright?"

"Yes, I'm fine, just tired. We got home about twenty minutes ago." Eddie sat in a chair. "I'll tell you about the trip when you come back."

"Is everything done?" There was a hesitation. "Did you do what you promised?"

"Yeah, I kept my promise. But it was his wife that did what was needed." Again, unlike Carl, he found himself unable to speak the words. But *did what was needed* made perfect sense to Cheryl.

Eddie paused and used his finger to push the ice cubes in his drink, then watched them pop to the surface, hearing them crack.

"I'm so happy you didn't have to do it. Aren't you?"

"I guess." He gulped his drink. "But Juan didn't come home, so we'll be going to San Antonio for a couple of days."

"My God, Eddie, I'm so sorry." There was a short pause. "But you're okay, right? You're not hurt, are you? Is Vinh hurt?"

"We're all fine. Vinh is fine, and I'm fine. Don't worry. Look, I'm tired and we still need to eat dinner. I'll call again tomorrow."

"You better. I love you. I miss you."

"Kiss the boys for me. I love you too." Eddie placed the handset into the cradle and downed the rest of his drink in a single slug.

Before everyone crashed for the night, Eddie made sandwiches and soup. The three men ate in silence.

•

After waking early, Eddie headed for the kitchen to brew the coffee. As he walked down the hall, he heard snoring coming from both bedrooms. He decided to let them sleep; there were no plans for today.

When he finished his second cup of coffee, Eddie went to the van, opened the unlocked passenger door, and found Juan's photo album.

Back in the kitchen, Eddie threw the album on the table and opened it as he drank another cup of coffee. On the first page he found an enlarged picture of the squad: Bear, Cain, Little JJ, Carl, Ray, and a younger version of himself stared back. His eyes glistened as he absorbed his brothers' youthful images.

Flipping through the pages, he studied each photograph.

The memories of the men he served with in war flooded his thoughts. Some were happy, and some created the nightmares he lived with every single night. The pleasant recollections, small incidents of humor and togetherness, jostled for space against the memories of all the terrible scenes he had witnessed through the years, the screams, the dying throes of good men. Fat tears rolled down his cheeks as if he'd never grieved for the fallen before this day. Maybe he hadn't.

He had been holding on to too much anger.

Now, he could let it go and let the tears come.

Eddie closed the album and slid his chair back to top off the cup. A voice startled him, causing him to spill coffee on the counter.

"Good morning. You're up early." Carl stood in the doorway. "Okay, bud?"

"Damn, Carl, give a man some warning that you're coming."

Eddie wiped up the mess then wiped his damp, tear stained face with a napkin. It was an embarrassment to be caught in such a state.

"What's got you so jumpy?" Carl placed a hand on Eddie's shoulder.

Eddie sighed. "Everything, man. I got the album you found in Juan's car. Check it out." He pointed at the table. "Want coffee?"

"Yeah, I do." Carl pulled out a chair and opened the book.

Eddie set the cup next to Carl.

Carl looked up. "Thanks." He turned a page. "Man, I can't believe these pictures."

"What's going on?" Vinh strolled into the kitchen.

"Nothing." Eddie held out the coffee pot. "You want coffee?"

Vinh opened the refrigerator door. "No, thanks. Getting a Coke."

When Vinh sat at the table, Carl pointed at a picture.

"Look at this one. It's you and Mama-san." He glanced at Vinh. "Damn, you were only a child."

Eddie looked over his shoulder.

"Yes, he was a child, but he'd already lived a lifetime compared to most men when someone took that photo."

He squeezed Vinh's shoulder.

Vinh studied the photo for a moment. "Yes, I was. Mama-san was a kind, caring woman." Vinh wiped at a tear. "I hardly remember what it's like to live in Vietnam. It's been so long."

"I'll be back in a minute." Eddie left the room headed for his bedroom. When he returned, Eddie slid a card onto the table.

"Here you go. Juan's mother's number." He looked at Carl. "You'll want to make the call."

"I can if you want me to. But you probably should make the call. You were the boss here." Carl's lips tugged downward. "Your project. It's your responsibility." He slid his chair out and stood.

Eddie's face was like thunder.

"Shit, man, all the way through this thing, you insisted on being the team leader, the one in control. Do this, don't do that . . . and now you're stepping down, just like that, 'cause you don't want to make the call?"

"It's not like that. Whatever way you look at it, you called on us for this job. So that makes it your job. Hell, the cops will have called her by now anyway."

"I know. But we should attend the funeral." Eddie ran his hand through his hair. "Don't you agree that we should go to say goodbye to him? And not just that, but do the decent thing by his mother, at least?"

Carl poured coffee into his cup. "Yeah, I do. You call, and we'll go."

Eddie lifted the handset from the cradle. He knew that death wasn't kind, especially when it took good people who were far too young. Juan didn't deserve to die. A mother shouldn't have to bury her son.

As he dialed the number, Eddie felt the guilt gnawing at his gut. If he had done things differently, Juan might have lived. He pushed the last button, and the phone rang.

"Hello, the Jackson residence," a female voice answered.

"Good morning, Mrs. Jackson. I'm Eddie Henderson, a friend of Juan's." Eddie stood in front of the window.

Carl and Vinh intently watched Eddie's face as he spoke.

"Yes, Eddie. Juan talked about you all the time." She started to cry. "I don't know if you heard, but my Juan's dead."

Eddie tried to sound shocked.

"That's why I'm calling. I heard about it on the news. What happened?"

"Killed in Houston two days ago. The funeral is tomorrow." She sobbed into the receiver. "Will you come? It's short notice, but I'd like that. And if you can, bring—"

She broke down.

"Yes, ma'am, I will be there. Wouldn't miss it for anything. I'm bringing two friends that knew Juan too."

After Eddie got all the details, he hung up the phone. "How about a drink?" He pulled three glasses and the bottle of Jim Beam from the cabinet.

SAYING GOODBYE

The caravan of cars pulled into the National Cemetery. Carl parked the van behind the last of the family vehicles. The three climbed out and strode to the gravesite.

There were dozens of people gathered around Juan's grave. Eddie noticed that an Army Honor Guard was standing near the flag-draped coffin. A bugler stood at attention next to some trees not far from the gravesite.

This was the first military funeral he'd attended. He often wondered how loved ones said goodbye when one of his brothers was sent home in a body bag.

Eddie observed that most people were stopping to talk to an older woman who sat near the casket. He walked toward her.

"Mrs. Jackson?"

She glanced up at him. "Yes, I am." Her face was flushed and her eyes were surrounded by dark circles. "Are you here for Juan?"

Carl and Vinh walked up behind Eddie. "Yes, I'm Eddie." He turned and pointed. "This is Carl and Vinh. Close friends of Juan's." He fought back the tears. "Listen, I'm sorry about Juan."

He leaned down and hugged Mrs. Jackson.

The veterans of war stood erect on that crisp December afternoon, their faces bearing deep creases as they acknowledged the loss of their brother. The sun shone brightly on the flag-draped casket.

Eddie thought how they had been through hell together. He remembered how they'd watched comrades, their brothers, die in combat. Now they were here to bury a brother who fought the demons he'd brought home from war, and lost.

A priest said what he needed to say to give some peace. The family wept.

On cue, seven members of the firing party, dressed in blues, aimed upward and fired three rifle volleys. The twenty-one-gun salute tradition came from battle ceasefires, when each side would remove the dead then fire three volleys indicating the dead were cleared.

A fitting honor for Juan, thought Eddie.

After a moment of silence, the bugler played Taps. While the sound echoed across the cemetery, goosebumps crept across every inch of Eddie's skin as tears rolled down his cheeks. He thought of Juan and how, after all that comradeship, all they had been through as a team, he had died alone. Guilt surged through his veins.

After the last note faded, the Honor Guard ceremoniously folded the American flag thirteen times with a triangular blue field of stars on top.

Carrying the flag, the senior member knelt in front of Mrs. Jackson. His voice resounded loud and clear.

"On behalf of the President of the United States, the United States Army, and a grateful nation, please accept this flag as a symbol of our appreciation for your loved one's honorable and faithful service." He presented the flag to her.

She struggled to smile as she accepted it, but it was small consolation. Mrs. Jackson buried her agonized face into the stars and stripes.

The soldier stayed with her, attempting to console the mother who had lost her only son.

Eddie choked on tears and grief as he watched the presentation. Before he left, Eddie silently stepped forward and gently touched the casket, saying his most profound, fondest goodbye to Juan.

Carl and Vinh did the same.

No man was afraid to show his tears.

As they walked toward the van, Eddie thought of the funerals that his brothers—Mitch Drexler, Ronnie Porter, Sergeant Stahl, Ray Laurel, Bear, and Cain—had after they were killed in 'Nam. He hoped they'd had the same tributes that Juan received. He imagined their family members receiving the flag that had draped over their caskets. "It doesn't seem enough."

"What?" Carl asked.

Eddie turned to look back at Juan's gravesite. "Nothing. Just thinking out loud."

•

Once home again at Eddie's, the three friends said their goodbyes as they stood outside the van.

Eddie gave Carl a tight bear hug. "I'll miss you. Thank you for coming when I needed you, buddy. And you were the best Team Leader. I realize now that I couldn't have done it. Probably would have fucked it up somehow."

Carl pushed Eddie away. "Come on, man, enough of that stuff." He smiled and punched Eddie on the arm. "We need to get together more often and under different circumstances."

"Let's do that." Eddie took a step backward.

Next, Carl embraced Vinh. After a couple of seconds, he released his hold. "Look after that old man, kid."

"I will." Vinh chuckled.

After Carl climbed into the driver's seat, he shut the door and rolled down the window. He looked at Eddie and Vinh as he turned the key in the ignition, bringing the engine alive again. When the vehicle was in gear, he pulled away from the curb, driving toward the interstate.

As he watched the van drive away, Eddie realized that Carl came in his time of need, without hesitation. It wasn't just because he hated Dang too. He came because of the bond they shared, a bond between two soldiers. They had a foundation of trust—no questions asked. You always took the leap to help a brother. Tears filled Eddie's eyes yet again.

Once the van disappeared, the two men went inside the house. Eddie flopped into his recliner as Vinh plugged in the Christmas lights. He stepped back to look at the tree, then sprawled on the couch.

"I like the Christmas season." Vinh stared at the tree. "Do you?"

"Yes, I love Christmas, especially with the boys." Eddie stood. "I'm going to call Cheryl." He went to the kitchen.

Eddie pulled down a glass and a bottle of bourbon. After making a drink, he sat at the kitchen table and stared out the window. Once he took a mouthful, he picked up the telephone and dialed the number.

"Hello," Cheryl answered.

"Hi honey, I'm back from Juan's funeral." He picked up his glass, twirling the ice.

"I was so worried about you and Vinh. I'm happy that you're home and all this is behind us now." Cheryl sighed. "How was his mother? She holding up okay?"

Eddie took a slow taste of the drink. "She didn't look well. Juan was her only child." He took another sip. "But she does have family around her for support."

"That's good. Family is important, especially at a time like this."

"Speaking of family, now that it's over, do you think you can come home Christmas day?" He twisted the phone cord as he gazed at the clear sky. "We can still have Christmas together. I miss you and the boys."

"I can do that. Mom and Dad can still spend Christmas morning with Mitch and Ronnie before we leave for home. I'll call you after I change the reservations."

Eddie smiled. "I love you. I'll let you get back to your parents."

"I love and miss you too. The boys and I can't wait to come home."

"See you in two days." Eddie stood with the handset in one hand and the drink in another, smiling with anticipation at the image of Cheryl coming home. He hung up the telephone.

After he refreshed his drink, Eddie sat at the table, lost in thought as he gazed out the window. For the first time in years, he felt free.

It was as if an inner peace had taken hold of his body since Dang and Canh died.

The years of war and the recent months of fighting and fearing Dang whirled around his mind like a tornado tearing through a cornfield. His thoughts moved from one year to another, flashing on the destruction, killing, and death he had witnessed.

He wondered if there was a way he could make up for all the things that war had made him do. Eddie wanted to become a better person, not a person that hunted and killed—but hopefully all that was behind him now. He didn't believe in a higher power; the war had taken that from him, but if there was one, then he wished for forgiveness.

WELCOME HOME

The blue Fairmont rolled to a stop in the driveway on the way back from the airport. Cheryl and the boys sprang from the car, running to the front door of their home. The three of them stood on the porch, giggling, waiting for the door to be unlocked. Eddie and Vinh carried the luggage, trailing behind Cheryl.

After he ruffled the boys' heads, Eddie unlocked the door and the family rushed inside. The children went directly to the pile of presents under the tree.

"Daddy, did Santa Claus come to our house?" Mitch asked.

Ronnie chimed in, "Did he, Daddy, did he?"

Eddie laughed. "You bet Santa came to our house. Who do you think brought those gifts? Mom and I can't afford all that."

Once the boys opened all the presents, they sat and played. An hour later, Cheryl tucked the kids into bed and then Eddie and Cheryl snuggled on the couch. He sat quietly, enjoying the warmth of her body next to him.

"I missed you," Eddie whispered. "The house was so empty without you in it."

She squeezed his hand. "I have something to tell you."

"Okay, I'm listening." Eddie looked into her eyes.

"I'm pregnant, and I'm naming him this time." Cheryl giggled.

"What, how do you know?" Eddie's eyes went wide.

Cheryl sat straight. "Okay, so I haven't been to the doctor yet, but I'm pretty sure."

"You said him. How do you know the baby is a boy?" Eddie searched her face for an answer.

She flashed a flirtatious smile. "If the baby is a boy, I'm naming him Eddie. I want to name him after you."

"I don't know what to say." Eddie kissed her on the lips and pulled her close to him. They sat quietly, enjoying the time with each other.

He imagined his future with Cheryl and their three sons. The images that played in his mind pulled him from the days gone by, the horror, death, and dying that came at night. Eddie decided to use the future to escape from the present and not let the past haunt him anymore.

He had his family and Vinh to share his life. Eddie wanted nothing more than to be finally free of the nightmares.

Eddie heard laughter coming from the bedrooms. "Okay, kids, come out here."

Mitch and Ronnie ran to the sofa, followed by Vinh.

The boys jumped onto their parents' laps while Vinh flopped next to Cheryl.

Eddie looked at his family, "I love you guys."

ABOUT THE AUTHOR

Glyn Haynie enlisted in the United States Army at the age of eighteen. His military career spanned twenty years, during which he served his country until his retirement in March of 1989. Glyn Haynie turned nineteen soon after arriving in Vietnam, where he found himself fighting with the Americal (23rd) Infantry Division. Before retiring, Haynie served as a drill instructor, a first sergeant and, finally, as an instructor for the US Army Sergeants Major Academy (USASMA).

After retiring from the army, Haynie earned an AAS degree in Management, a BS degree in Computer Information Systems, and an MA degree in Computer Resources and Information Systems. He worked as a software engineer/project manager for eight years before teaching at Park University as a full-time instructor. Haynie continued as an adjunct instructor for thirteen more years.

Glyn Haynie and his wife of thirty-three years, Sherrie, currently reside in Texas. They have five children, fourteen grandchildren, and four great-grandchildren. Three of their sons have served combat tours in either Iraq or Afghanistan. This is a family in which service to their country is a tradition.

To learn more about Glyn Haynie and his work, please visit his website:

http://www.glynhaynie.net
Email: glyn@glynhaynie.com

I hope you enjoyed this book. If so, would you do me a favor? Like all authors, I rely on online reviews, and your opinion is invaluable. Would you take a few moments now to share your assessment of my book on any book review website you prefer? Your opinion will help the book marketplace to become more transparent and useful to all.

Thank you much!
Glyn